Tessa moved her shoulders restlessly as she poked at her food. 'I'd decide when it was appropriate. And if *she* was old enough to understand, I'd tell the truth.'

Chase leaned close, so close Tessa could see the black flecks in his eyes.

'The truth? That he was made in a doctor's office and not a bedroom? That his father was some man he'll never know?'

His tone was intimate, husky and Tessa swallowed nervously. 'That can't be helped.'

'Yes, it can.'

'How——?' Her eyes widened instantly at the look of intent on his face. 'Oh, no!' She shook her head, looking scared. 'Don't—' she wiped her lips '—don't say it!'

'Marry me...'

AMY FETZER

was born in New England and raised all over the world. She uses her experiences, along with bits and pieces of the diverse people she's met, in creating the characters and settings for her novels. 'Nobody's safe,' she says. 'There are heroes and heroines right in front of us, if we just take the time to look.' Married nineteen years to a U.S. Marine and the mother of two sons, Amy covets the moments when she can curl up with a cup of cappuccino and a good book. Published previously in historical and time-travel novels and novellas, she happily steps into contemporary romance with her first Desire™ for Silhouette® Books, *Anybody's Dad*.

For my agent,
Irene Goodman
Thanks for tearing off my blinders and
seeing this one coming before I did.

One

"**I**t's too late, Chase."

"What do you mean?" he said into the phone, an edge to his voice. Lawyers had an annoying habit of dragging out the details, especially for their friends.

"The procedure took. Six months ago."

"What! You mean there's a woman walking around with my baby inside her and I've never laid eyes on her?"

"That about sums it up."

Chase Madison shielded his eyes from the sun blasting through his office window and rubbed his temples. Janis had done this. He just knew it. "God, if Janis wasn't already dead, I'd kill her."

"Oh, it gets better."

Chase closed his eyes, tamping down his temper. "Let's have it."

"She believes you're nothing but a sperm donor." Something nasty twisted inside Chase just then. "And she isn't going to let you near this child, nor give you the time of day."

"We'll just see about that."

Chase hung up the phone and sank into the nearest chair, cradling his aching head in his hands. *A sperm donor.* Wonderful. If his marriage alone wasn't the grand joke of the century, now he felt as if Janis were taking digs from the grave. Chase wasn't mourning her. He'd done that briefly months ago, after the accident, with whatever little feeling he had left for her. Now he felt only anger and resentment. She'd used her job at the fertility clinic to get back at him. She'd had access, and God knows she'd had motivation. But this, he thought, was beyond even her. This was vicious.

It always came back to kids. He wanted them. She couldn't have any. It hadn't mattered to him at the time. He just wanted to be a father. Anybody's father. He wanted to feel the sweet energy kids gave, their fascination for discovery, wanted to love them and feel loved. With secret dreams of his own son, he'd convinced Janis to go the adoption route—a seven-year wait for a newborn. But it was Janis, as administrator for the clinic, who'd introduced the possibility of a surrogate mother.

Chase hadn't liked the idea of a strange woman having his child by artificial insemination. Even the sound of it was clinically impersonal. And he couldn't imagine a woman going through pregnancy and childbirth only to relinquish her rights to her baby. But Janis had convinced him it was reasonable. Persuaded him with the fact that the child would at least have Chase's blood in his veins.

You let her convince you, his conscience niggled. He'd wanted a child that badly, yet still he'd dragged his heels. He remembered the humiliation of entering a little sterilized room, staring at the specimen cup in his hand, the leather office couch, the stack of video tapes on the TV/VCR. Then he'd dragged Janis in with him. She was very accommodating about assisting him, as he recalled.

Two weeks later his world fell apart. Or at least what he thought was his marriage. Hell. It had been over before that, he knew. Just as he knew having children was the wrong reason to hold a marriage together. Yet he'd felt cheated out of something precious and wonderful when he'd found the birth control pills tucked in the glove box of her car when he'd taken it to the shop. Janis wasn't infertile. She'd just never wanted children. Never wanted her career or her figure or her life interrupted. Let the baby machines do it, she'd said, unaware that he'd heard her bitter comments until he stepped around the edge of her office door. Oh, she'd stumbled through an explanation, but in that moment, he'd seen her for what she truly was. Selfish, heartless, a lousy example of impending motherhood. He'd told her to dump their files, their marriage and his donation.

Obviously she hadn't. He'd known she was bitter, but this? Manipulating files and specimens? Why?

For a baby.

His baby.

An incredible warmth crept into his chest, seeping out to his limbs. Chase sagged back into the leather chair and savored the feeling, knowing it wouldn't last, wouldn't stay. Had she intentionally allowed the surrogate-intended sperm to go to a woman who thought she was selecting only genes and chromosomes from a bank? Was she bitter enough to see the child he longed for created, only to keep the baby from his grasp? He hated to think anyone was that horrible.

Leaning forward, he scooted the pad of paper closer and read the name. The woman wasn't even one of the potential surrogates they'd interviewed.

Tessa Lightfoot.

She wanted a child, but didn't want the father.

Well, Miss Lightfoot. You got both. And she couldn't dump him down the drain with the rest of the liquid papas.

Tessa gripped the phone, praying she'd heard wrong. "This can't be happening. Tell me it isn't."

"It is, Sis. Now stay calm."

"I am calm!"

"Oh, sure."

"Dia, please," Tessa moaned, blinking back fresh tears.

"As your counsel, I advise you to meet with him."

"No way." She plucked a tissue from a lace-covered box and blotted her eyes.

"Tessa, listen," Dia said in a calm tone that always soothed Tessa. One would think she was the elder sister. "He's not an ogre."

"Have you met him?" Warts and baldness immediately came to mind.

"No, just his lawyer."

"You guys run like a wolf pack, so that doesn't count."

"He has rights." Dia's voice was tight.

"No, he doesn't. This baby is mine, all mine. Selecting sperm from a bank was supposed to insure that. If I wanted a father around I would have gone the conventional route."

"And you selected his. Why?"

"Oh, that hardly matters now. It's the clinic's fault, let him sue them."

"He's not suing. He wants to be a part of his child's life."

Panic raced through Tessa. "Never. Do you hear me, Dia? Never!"

"Tessa, sit."

Tessa sat, a soft plop onto a stack of floor pillows.

"Most men get the hell scared out of them when it comes to pregnancy and babies." Like her ex, Tessa thought, flipping her braid back over her shoulder. "Perhaps he just wants to offer financial support?" Dia finished.

Tessa made a face, then glanced around her cozy little house. "I don't need it."

"I know, but give him the chance to do the right thing. If you don't, this could get ugly."

A judge, the media, she realized, her child given an initial like Baby M. "Okay, okay. I will, under protest. One meeting and that's it."

"Tomorrow morning at nine. My office."

Tessa's brows knitted softly. "You were so sure I'd say yes?"

"You pay me to know what you need before you need it."

"Living in the same house for twenty years didn't hurt either, huh?"

Dia's laughter filtered through the phone, making Tessa smile as she said goodbye. Flicking off the cordless phone and tossing it aside, Tessa sank deeper into the mound of pillows, spread-eagle. Toeing off her sandals, she stared at the bordered ceiling, smoothing her hands over her belly. The baby moved in a slow, rolling wave, and she touched every ripple, smiling to herself, gaining strength. She wasn't going to let this *person,* this entity she refused to give a face to, get to her. This baby was hers, extra special, extra loved and extra wanted, because when she was young and married to Ryan, she'd had her chance and lost it.

Her ex hadn't wanted to be a father, ever, and although he'd said often enough that *she* was all he needed, she chose not to believe him. Disillusionment and hard reality hit when her birth control failed and he gave her a choice—abort or divorce. The confrontation had ended her marriage and she realized her own naiveté had allowed it to happen. The foolishness of youth, she thought. But miscarrying in the middle of her divorce had devastated her the most. Tessa's eyes burned suddenly and she stroked her belly, taking deep calming breaths. Just thinking about how Ryan had come rushing back when he'd heard about the miscarriage still upset her. She'd lived on her anger then, focusing on her career, on becoming financially independent enough to afford a child, *without* a father.

She'd almost waited too long.

But now, she was exactly where she wanted to be. And she'd fight this faceless enemy with everything she had before giving into the *donor's* arrogant demands to be a part of *her* baby's life.

"We'll get through this," she whispered to her unborn child.

This Chase Madison didn't know what he was up against when he faced a mother protecting her child.

Two

Chase stood near the office window, his back to his lawyer, Tigh McBain, and stared out the spotless glass, watching the traffic move on the streets below. His breath almost made frost, it was so cool in the long conference room, and he checked his watch for the third time.

"She's late."

"Tessa's always late," a soft voice said, and he turned to see a small, slender young woman enter the conference room. She greeted Tigh politely, setting her briefcase on the long table as her secretary, a man for God's sake, followed her, placing a coffee service and a pitcher of water on the table.

"And you tolerate it?"

She met his gaze, and Chase saw the shark beneath the impeccably tailored attorney. "Sisters have a tendency to tolerate a lot from each other."

Sisters. Wonderful. Nothing like having her family forces joined against him.

"I'm Dia Lightfoot." Chase looked her over thoroughly,

and she seemed to expect it, an odd smile crossing her lips. She was attractive, severe in appearance, businesslike in a fitted Chanel suit, black hair whipped tightly into a twist. Everything about Ms. Dia Lightfoot spoke of a professional hardness he saw too often in women climbing the corporate ladder. But to Chase, every lawyer was a shark, including Tigh. God, was this what awaited him? A woman so unable to spare a moment from her demanding career that she chose a sperm bank instead of taking the time for a relationship? His stomach knotted and he returned his gaze out the window, hands braced behind his back. He rocked on his heels, flinching when a buzzer sounded. He glanced back to see Ms. Lightfoot flip a cellular phone and speak softly, then click it off and drop it into her briefcase.

"She's on her way up."

Chase didn't think his stomach could clench any tighter. He wasn't noticing the magnificent skyline, or his chilled skin. His imagination was too busy painting an unpleasant picture of Dia's sister. A duplicate of the shark in heels, he thought. Gritty. Clinical enough to breed her baby in a doctor's office.

A rap on the door sounded, and Chase turned as the secretary pushed open the heavy wood, then stepped aside.

Chase's brows rose high on his forehead as a very pregnant woman moved gracefully into the icy room. His conjured images were instantly destroyed as she seemed to float to her sister, hugging her. Not a brief touch of cheeks, but a real, loving hug. The temperature rose, warming the room. And Chase couldn't take his eyes off her or her rounded tummy. That's my baby in there, he thought, then brought his gaze to her face. He noticed the small straw hat first, the rolled brim, fanned back over one ear, her long black hair tucked behind and falling down her back. Her obviously pregnant body was clothed in a flowing cream silk and lace creation reaching mid-calf. The dress was shapeless, yet the simple garment draped her like a mystery, showing curves and showing nothing. Bet she never strapped herself into suits and heels, he thought, pleased and wary. His gaze immediately dropped to her legs as if whether or not she wore high heels would make a difference, yet he found matching opaque stockings and shoes that looked more like ballet slippers. Even her feet were delicate.

Tessa Lightfoot was femininity at its finest.

And he was sunk.

How was he supposed to fight this? This ethereal image of motherhood.

She smiled, but he only caught half of it, her face turned away as her counsel introduced her to his. Tigh flashed her his easy grin, then offered her a chair, and she sat, clutching her tiny beaded handbag on her lap before she finally twisted a look at him.

Chase nodded.

Tessa nodded.

The air between them was charged with defiance before Tessa turned back to Dia, taking a calming breath. Oh, lord. Did he have to be so handsome? Where were the warts she spent half the night praying for? she wondered as his lawyer gestured to an empty chair and Chase rounded the back of the table, sliding in it. He adjusted his tie and let his gaze creep across the table and up to her face. She could feel it, like a fingertip under her chin, and she fought the urge to look at him. She kept her gaze locked on Dia.

Her lawyer racked papers and addressed Tigh. "Miss Lightfoot wants to know what rights you believe you're entitled to."

"I don't *believe* I am, I know."

Tessa looked at him sharply, briefly, and in a heartbeat, Chase was snagged in those vivid green eyes.

"Miss Lightfoot feels this is the clinic's problem."

Ignoring Tigh's prior warning to let him negotiate, Chase went on. "It's *our* problem. Because that's *our* baby. And does Miss Lightfoot," he growled, "even have a voice?"

Tessa cocked a look at him. "As a matter of fact I do, though not as loud as yours."

Chased stared, then grinned suddenly, and Tessa was startled, her cheeks warming.

Dia and Tigh exchanged a glance.

"Surely your client will agree this is an unusual situation," Tigh said. "We would like to know how this mistake was discovered."

The lawyers exchanged copies of paperwork. "Lab techs were updating records, a periodic checking of log numbers against donors, making certain no donor is used more than once." Chase felt his skin tighten. "The donor's—" Dia cleared her throat, making Chase squirm "—Mr. Madison's—sperm was incorrectly listed."

"Then how do they know he's the one," Tigh asked, "if he was just a number in a registry?"

Dia glanced at Tessa and she nodded.

"When this matter arose, Miss Lightfoot underwent amniocentesis to be certain."

That she would go through such pain and risk told Chase more than he wanted to know and he leaned across the table, his gaze flicking between Dia and Tigh, then to Tessa.

"And?" His breath locked in his lungs.

Tessa knew this should come from her and lifted her gaze from her lap, her eyes glossed with unshed tears. She put just enough resentment into her tone as she said, "It was your donation, Mr. Madison."

The wind went out of Chase then. There had been the shadow, the sliver of a chance that this was just a mix-up in paperwork. But now that warm feeling came again, spreading to his fingers this time, seeping into his heart and burrowing deeper and stronger with each passing moment. A dad. He leaned back in the chair, so damned pleased. And he hoped it showed, hoped this woman realized that he wasn't giving up any rights to his child, without one hell of a fight.

But Tessa knew, by his expression, his eyes, warming to a wonderful cobalt blue. She looked away suddenly. *Oh, God, what have I done?* Acknowledging him offered him rights. Parental rights. No. He's just the donor, a test tube of defrosted fluid.

"The difficulty lies in how your sperm was even registered," Dia was saying. "As I understand it, you and your wife—" Tessa looked instantly horrified and Chase interrupted sharply.

"Ex-wife. Dead ex-wife." Bitter, a quick slap of fury before it was gone.

"I'm sorry, Mr. Madison," both women said, but Chase had eyes only for Tessa, his gaze burning over her golden skin as he stared and stared, until she lifted her eyes to his. A small smile curved his lips, half there, half not, and it made her wonder what was hatching in his brain.

"You were going to use a surrogate," Dia finished, and Tigh agreed for him. "Well, while Mr. Madison's specimen should have been destroyed at the termination of his marriage, my client was listed as a surrogate."

Tessa jerked her gaze to her sister. "That's impossible."

"Is it?" Chase interjected.

She turned on Chase. "Yes, I would never have a child only to give it away, not for anyone." Her voice rose. "And Dr. Faraday knows this, knows exactly what I've been through!" Dia clasped her hand and Tessa fell into silence.

Chase's heart suddenly skittered. Was there a problem with the pregnancy? Though he wanted to know, needed to know, he didn't think she'd tell him if he asked.

"I will never give you my baby," she asserted, her beautiful eyes sparking with barely checked fury.

"Our baby," he countered across the table.

"No. Mine. The donor signed over rights when he donated sperm to the bank. That's why I chose it."

"Don't like men, do you?"

Tessa looked appalled and Chase had his answer.

"Regardless," their lawyers interrupted, sending their clients an I'm-supposed-to-do-the-talking look. Chase and Tessa settled back, stiff, their anger sizzling across the polished table.

"You both have rights. Suing the clinic will not change anything," came from Dia.

"I don't want to sue," Chase said.

"Then we can set up visitation rights when the child is born."

Chase's gaze jerked to her attorney's. "No way. I'm not *visiting* my own child. I want him."

Panic, absolute and undeniable, sent Tessa leaning forward, her hand gripping the table ledge. "I don't want you in my life, Mr. Madison, father or not!" She stood abruptly. "Possession is nine-tenths of the law, and until this child is born, you have no rights."

"I have the same as any father."

"Then go off and be anybody's father. *We* don't want you."

Dia rose and settled Tessa back into the chair, glaring at Chase. "It isn't wise to upset her," she remarked.

"Oh Dia, be serious," Tessa murmured under her breath. "I'm pregnant, not an invalid."

"Use any weapon you can," her sister whispered, and Tessa scowled.

"I think the court should decide this," Tigh suggested.

"No!" came from both parents, nearly bringing them out of their chairs.

Dia and Tigh glanced at each other, then their clients. The lawyers leaned their heads together, speaking softly, and Chase gazed at Tessa. She was fuming mad and he liked it. Even though she was going to fight him in every way she could, he liked it. She was protecting her baby, their baby. But he was just as determined to get what he wanted. His gaze lowered to her fingers drawing slow circles over her tummy, and Chase suddenly wondered what those fingers would feel like on his skin.

Damn.

Where did that come from?

Yet he watched her, the slight tremble in her breath, the way the force of the air conditioning fluttered the delicate fabric of her dress against her breast. She was truly a radiant woman, and he wondered, as any normal man would, what she looked like without his child growing so beautifully inside her.

"Have lunch with me, Miss Lightfoot?"

She blinked, stunned, then her green eyes narrowed. "Why?"

"Don't you think it would be better for all three of us—" he nodded to her stomach, "—if we came to at least a cease of friendly fire?"

Caught in indecision, Tessa let her gaze linger over him, his rugged features, his dark brown hair, short and cleanly cut, his eyes, blue as a kid's crayon and penetrating. But mostly, aside from the body in the dark suit, she noticed the lines around those incredible eyes, tanned and crimped and showing Tessa that this man, gruff and angry, smiled. A lot.

"All right." She nodded almost regally. "Cease-fire agreement. I promise not to throw food at you, at least."

Chase's lips tugged at the corners and he folded his arms over his chest, briefly glancing at the floor to hide a smile, but all Tessa noticed was the straining fabric, the muscles hiding beneath the tailored coat. Too sexy for his own good, and she imagined he knew it.

"I'll meet you at noon at—" she paused, looking thoughtful. "Golden—"

"Arches?" he teased.

"No, Dragon. I want dim sum."

Chase eyed her, her wonderful belly, then her face. "Cravings, Miss Lightfoot?"

"No. Hunger. Humor me, I'm pregnant," she said, then stood, kissed her sister's cheek, and nodded to Tigh before she left. Chase looked from Dia, who was smiling royally, to Tigh, who smiled consistently, then to the empty chair. He bolted for the door and the lawyers dropped back into their chairs.

"I feel as if I've cheated my client," Tigh said.

"Me, too."

"We didn't do anything."

Dia sent him a sly glance. "Oh, I think we did."

At the elevator Chase caught her, pressed the down button and grinned.

"I said noon."

"Where are you going?"

"If it's any of your business, back to work."

"Work?"

"What? Did you think I was independently wealthy? That I could have a baby when I felt like it?"

He shook his head, jamming his hands in his trouser pockets and ruining the fine lines of the suit. "I don't know what to think."

"Good."

His lips thinned. "Try not to fire on a white flag," he said through gritted teeth.

Tessa sighed heavily. "Look, Mr. Madison—"

"Chase."

"Mr. Madison," she stressed. "You may have contributed to the gene pool, but that's it."

"Are you going to hold the fact that I can't give birth against me?"

She reared back. "Of course not. But we don't have anything to say to each other, and I'd like to keep it that way. Lunch is a compromise."

"You mean a concession to the lowly father, huh?"

God, it sounded so insensitive and spiteful when he put it like that.

"I'm meaningless to you, aren't I?" he continued. "You couldn't care less if I spend the next ten years trying to gain my rights."

The elevator chimed and the door sprang open. She stepped inside and Chase stood still as she faced him and punched the lobby button. The moments between gave her a chance to forget his hurt look and retrieve her determination. He didn't want to simply help financially as Dia suspected. Chase Madison wanted her baby and he was planning to make her life miserable.

"Forget about me, Mr. Madison. The last thing I want is *you* in my baby's life."

The door closed and Chase jerked his tie loose, then shoved his fingers through his hair. Not the baby's life, he thought angrily, or yours?

Tessa watched him from a distance, gathering her nerve. He'd changed into more casual clothes, and she remembered how he'd kept tugging at his tie earlier that morning. He either didn't wear suits often or just didn't like them, she decided. She watched him as he stared off into the street. The sidewalk café was a good spot, open, crowded. They couldn't argue here. Yet it struck her that he looked lonely, forgotten, relaxed in the chair, one arm slung over the back. Women paraded past him, hoping, she didn't doubt, to catch his attention. But he didn't spare them a glance, his gaze so distant she felt a pang of sympathy. He was divorced, his wife dead, and he lived alone. That's all Dia had been able to find out in such a short time, other than that he owned a construction company.

And you want to take his child away from him, a voice pestered. She moved her shoulder as if to nudge it away. *He wants to take my baby. Mine.* This child had been all hers, until last week, until *his* lawyer called, until computer glitches and the damn clinic made it his, too.

Liar, the voice cried. *Liar. He is the biological father.*

Tessa rubbed the space between her eyes, willing back the threat of a headache, and straightened her shoulders. Nodding to the maître d', she followed him to the table. As if sensing her presence, Chase turned his head, then leapt to his feet, pulling out a chair. She sank into it gratefully, working off her shoes. Pregnancy and happy feet did not coexist.

She smelled like cinnamon, Chase decided as he tucked her chair and took his seat. They ordered, and when the waiter left, Chase turned his attention to the woman across from him. He'd positioned her chair at a safe distance, sensing she didn't want to be too close, and he didn't want to scare her off. The stakes were too high. She could vanish, taking his unborn child with her, and Chase would be left alone. Again.

"Are you just going to stare at me or what?"

His gaze lingered over her dress. It was the same one she'd worn earlier that morning, and he was glad she hadn't changed. He liked the antique look. It suited her.

"Where do you work, Tessa?" he asked

She thought about saying nothing, but with Tigh McBain for a lawyer, Chase likely knew the shade of her bathroom by now.

"I have a shop about four blocks from here, *Mr. Madison*," she enunciated, hoping he caught her meaning.

He did, but ignored it. "Let me guess, a dress shop."

"No, an everything shop. Tessa's Attic."

He frowned.

"I design and manufacture period clothing—Victorian, Gatsby." She gestured to her own clothes. "Along with the proper accoutrements," she added.

She works with her hands, too, he thought, his gaze shifting to her long, carefully manicured fingers, then to the dress again, skimming the delicate grape lace worked with pearls and tiny ribbons. It looked as if air held it together, and it made him think of all those wonderful sexy bits of lingerie women wore to drive men insane. No wonder it suited her so well. He found himself wanting to see her before she was pregnant or after, without the huge tummy. He wanted to see Tessa without anything at all.

Tessa felt his gaze, saw it darken and deepen, sending an unfamiliar heat through her already warm blood. Hot flashes, that's all, she thought. The waiter came and placed food before them. Tessa, caught in Chase's gaze, still didn't realize their lunch had arrived until she nearly dropped the dim sum in her lap.

"Who hurt you?" His words came softly, like a warm caress.

She didn't like it. "I beg your pardon?"

"Who hurt you so badly that you don't want a man in your life?"

A lie would have done nicely right now, but Tessa couldn't get it past her lips. "It's not that I don't want one. Rather I've found it...unnecessary. I do fine alone, with an occasional date."

"Why didn't you just sleep with some poor schmuck and walk away? You'd have exactly what you wanted then."

"No. I wouldn't," she replied tightly. "I wasn't going to risk a disease or anything else. What should I have done? Ah, excuse me—" she poked the air with her chopsticks "—could you be tested for diseases so I can get pregnant? Hurry though, I'm ovulating." He smiled at that. "I couldn't do that anyway, at least not and keep it from him."

"But you would from me?"

She put down her chopsticks and rubbed her temple. "It's different. I went into this with the assurance that the donor would never know. Donors sign away their rights."

"Unless the kid wants to find them."

She shrugged.

"What were you going to tell my son when he asked about his father?"

Again, her shoulders moved restlessly as she poked at her food. "I'd decide when it was appropriate. And if she was old enough to understand, I'd tell the truth."

Abruptly he leaned close, hemming in the air, the moment. The man was so close she could see the black flecks in his eyes.

"The truth? That he was made in a doctor's office and not a bedroom? That his father was some man he'll never know?"

His tone was intimate, husky, and Tessa swallowed nervously. "That can't be helped."

"Yes, it can."

"How—?" Her eyes widened instantly at the look of intent on his face. "Oh, no!" She shook her head, looking scared. "Don't—" she wiped her lips "—don't say it!"

"Marry me."

She stood abruptly, throwing down her napkin. "That never fixes anything, especially this."

Chase rose slowly. "Tessa, calm down."

"I am calm," she insisted. "I said lunch. Talk. Not a damn proposal that isn't warranted." She left the table, angry, stomping, then froze, looking down at her stock-inged feet. Chase watched her shoulders sag as she turned back. Dropping into the chair, he fought a smile as she stepped into her shoes and grabbed her purse.

He caught her and a tingling sang up his arm. "Tessa, wait. Talk to me."

"No." She wiggled free. "Talk is doing—" She gasped suddenly, gripping his shoulder and clutching her belly.

Chase tensed, his gaze shooting between her face and the baby. In a heartbeat he realized she wasn't in pain, but that his child, his baby, was moving wildly inside her. Without thought, he pulled her onto his lap, his hand covering the rolling pokes and ripples.

The audacity of the man, Tessa thought, struggling to get up, but he held her down. Then Tessa went still as glass, watching his expression—awed and happy. Deliriously happy. And she felt it like a sweet fragrance on the breeze, almost tangible.

"Chase," she whispered, and he lifted his gaze. Her heart nearly broke. His eyes, dark, haunting eyes that could almost pierce through her, were damp and soft and so un-believably vulnerable she thought she'd drown in them. He looked helpless and his fingers flexed on her belly, follow-ing the motion lower. A burning, familiar and sensual and heady, spilled through her body. She shifted on his lap and he dropped his gaze to her tummy.

"That's incredible," he whispered, a catch in his voice, and it hit her that he hadn't understood exactly what he was fighting over. A human being. Genes and syringes aside, there was life inside her and he was just recognizing how very real it all was. That this wasn't a battle for rights and territory, but a battle over a baby. A tiny, helpless baby.

Tessa was fast losing perspective. The heat of his touch

and the savage look in his eyes chiseled at the courage she needed. In the space of a few moments, the man fought with her, proposed to her, then showed her a side of himself she never imagined he possessed. And she felt as if she'd just stepped off a roller coaster—dizzy, unstable. It scared her, this jumble of feelings, and as Chase applied pressure to her back, urging her close, she recognized want and hunger and need in herself. She was pregnant; she wasn't supposed to feel this way, was she? Yet still she leaned into him, still she let him touch her belly, still she ignored the customers whispering around them.

When Tessa covered his hand with hers, Chase felt emotion stir in him, a thick heaviness in his chest he hadn't experienced in all his thirty-five years. Unborn life poked at his palm. It was his child, letting him know he was there, involved, yet a separate entity from the mother. This child is a living, breathing part of me too, he thought. *Me.* And the baby needed him. His gaze moved over Tessa's belly, then up her body to her face, and she smiled tenderly. God, she was beautiful. And she was doing things to him, intoxicating things, with her buttocks tucked into his lap, the scent of her perfume and her skin, the look in her eyes. For an instant, Chase saw her in his bed, naked and damp and wanting. His hand at her back spread, moving upward, drawing her closer. His breath brushed her warm lips. So sweet.

Her eyes blinked open and she jerked back. "No. No, no, no." She pushed off his lap, scrambling for her purse, ignoring his help and repeating "no" over and over as she left him and the restaurant as quickly as she could. Chase watched her go, sinking into the chair. She couldn't have moved any faster if her life depended on it, and he smiled, silly and sappy. Several customers joined him.

"My baby," he said, gesturing, then leaned forward and braced his arms on the table, catching his breath. She felt it. God, he prayed she had experienced that electricity, because he felt fried down to his socks. And the only reason he didn't follow her was that the entire restaurant would know exactly what her squirming had done to him.

Three

———

Tessa slipped the purchase into a bag and handed it over to her customer, forcing her smile to remain in place as Miss Dewberry called out in her singsong voice from the dressing room.

"Coming," Tessa sang back, her shoulders drooping.

"I'll take care of her, Miss Lightfoot," one of her salesgirls, a college student, said.

"Thank you, but Miss Dewberry will only make you miserable, Dana," Tessa whispered. She'd find fault with everything the girl did, and Tessa didn't want her best clerk upset enough to leave. She needed her. Dana looked great in Tessa's designs and had a marvelous eye for window displays.

Dana conceded with a sour glance at the dressing rooms and turned away to assist another customer. Tessa snatched three more outfits off the rack and headed to the back of the store. She soothed the older woman's complaints and suggested another style. Tessa wouldn't put up with her moods if she didn't spend nearly a thousand dollars every

time she walked through the door. Besides, being unmar-
ried and childless at fifty must be hard. Though Tessa could
understand why the woman was alone. Her aura was brown,
as Tessa's mother would say.

"I think we should try a larger size," she suggested.
"This pattern may run a touch small," she added, for the
woman's expression was viperous. Tessa handed over the
garments and leaned back against the papered wall. She
wanted a nap. She wanted to put her feet up. And she almost cried when the door chime sounded again.

Sleep had eluded her last night, her mind constantly slipping to Chase, remembering the look in his eyes when he
felt the baby move and the wonderful scent of him just
before he kissed her. No, *nearly* kissed her, she reminded
herself.

She couldn't let him seduce her. Not that she believed
for a moment he was attracted to a pregnant woman with
swollen ankles. He just wanted his baby. *My baby*, she
corrected, refusing to be lured by his smiles and charm.

When Miss Dewberry popped out of the dressing room,
displeasure evident in her pinched expression, Tessa prepared herself for the criticism. Pushing away from the wall,
she inspected the fit, adjusting the delicate fabric over the
woman's ample figure.

"It scratches, and this isn't the French lace I like," Miss
Lila Dewberry sniped.

And the style is for a younger slimmer woman, Tessa
thought. Or hadn't the woman noticed the deep braless-cut
back?

"But what do you think of the color?"

Pink dress, red hair? Get a clue, Tessa thought.

"It doesn't do you justice," a masculine voice said, and
both women turned.

Tessa's heart did a strange flip at the sight of Chase
propped against the wide doorway, arms folded over his
flat stomach. His slight smile, so very masculine and seductive, practically simmered in the air. God, he looked

good, she thought, even in a simple blue T-shirt and very worn jeans.

"I beg your pardon?" Miss Dewberry said waspishly, and Tessa's gaze shifted between her source of sleeplessness and her immediate source of a headache.

"The color, I mean." He leaned back slightly and pulled a darker, more somber shade of the same dress from the rack and handed it to the woman. Tessa noticed it was a larger size. "This was made for you."

Miss Dewberry smiled, for the first time in centuries Tessa imagined, then swept into the dressing room.

Chase's gaze shifted to Tessa.

"Thank you," she said, then lowered her voice. "She was really beginning to wear on me."

"You look exhausted."

"I am." She collected the discarded garments, righting them on the hangers.

"Is that because of me?" he said with a grin.

Her eyes narrowed. "Yes. You and your imagined rights. What do you want, Mr. Madison?"

"For you to take it easy, for one thing."

"Me and my baby were doing just fine."

Until you, she was saying. His gaze slipped over her, the dark beige top and cleanly pressed slacks, but it was her face that showed her fatigue. Wisps of hair lay damp at her nape where she'd pulled the dark mass back in a wide bow. Shadows clung beneath her eyes, and a grayish pallor tinted her skin.

"Please leave my shop," she said, suddenly uncomfortable. She bent to retrieve a box of shoes, yet when she straightened, she staggered. Chase lurched, catching her, taking her weight.

She sagged against him, drawing her breath slowly, blinking, and Chase lifted her in his arms and carried her out of the dressing room area.

"I'm quite capable of walking," she said, squirming.

"You can hardly stand," came in a warning tone, and

she scowled at him. Her assistant looked up and raced to
them, opening the door to her office and letting him inside.

"Can I get a doctor?"

"No." Tessa was annoyed that Dana addressed Chase,
waiting for his command. The interfering man.

"Just water," Chase said, laying Tessa on the stuffed
couch. He tugged off her shoes as Dana filled a glass from
the cooler and brought it to him, then left, closing the door.

"I have to see to Miss Dewberry."

"That crabapple can wait."

"This is a business, Chase Madison, and I need hers."

She started to get up, but he pressed her gently back
down, handing her the glass before pulling a chair alongside the sofa. He sat. "Drink." When she looked as if she'd
rebel, he tipped the glass to her lips. She drank obediently.
"Are you hungry?"

"I never had the chance to eat it," she said, gesturing
to the meal on her desk, her breathing a little fast. Chase
stood and scooped up the sandwich and fruit, bringing it
back and setting it beside her on the sofa. "Eat."

"Eat. Drink," she grunted lowly. "Can't you do anything but bark at me?"

"Yes." His gaze swept her leisurely. "But I'll get to
that later," he said in the sexiest voice God could create,
and Tessa had to smile. He really was too handsome.

She bit into the sandwich half, moaning with pleasure,
and Chase wanted to hear more of it, when he kissed her
someday. The sandwich was gone in seconds, and as she
reached for the other half, Chase leaned back in the chair,
stretching out his legs. It amazed him how much he enjoyed
just watching her. She was totally focused on her food,
devouring it in minutes, drinking water, popping bits of
fruit into her lovely mouth. He didn't think she remembered
he was there until she frowned at the empty wrappers and
looked around as if searching for crumbs. He chuckled and
her gaze flew to his, a dull red creeping into her face.

Tessa wiped her mouth with a paper napkin and

shrugged. She wasn't going to make excuses for her appetite.

"Want me to get you more?"

"No, thank you. We're satisfied." She patted her stomach.

We. A package deal. Chase had racked his brains for a solution to their problem, but late last night, when only her fiery green eyes filled his mind, he realized that first he had to get to know her. Then they could do something about their child and the opposition they had.

Sitting here with her, taking care of her, felt so natural he wanted it to go on. However, the uncomfortable look on her face said she didn't want him around, ever. It stung, he admitted, and abruptly stood to refill her glass.

A rap on the door and Dana popped her head around the panel. Chase looked up, glancing between the girl and Tessa.

"I'm sorry, Miss Lightfoot, but Miss Dewberry is asking for you. I tried to explain, but I think she's going to leave."

Tessa straightened, swinging her legs off the couch.

"You stay put," Chase commanded, pointing at her, and Tessa froze. He looked at the salesgirl. "Tell Miss Dewberry to keep her shorts on. I'll take care of her."

"You?" both women squeaked, stunned.

"Yes, dammit, me." He waved Dana on, then turned to Tessa, lifting her legs back onto the couch.

"I have to get back to her."

His gaze darkened. She looked more ready to sleep than work. "Let her wait."

"Chase Madison, this is my shop, my livelihood, and that woman—" she pointed to the door "—no matter how finicky she can be, is a very good paying customer."

He towered over her, forcing her to crane her neck to look up at him. His body blocked the light, blocked any escape, and she felt like a prisoner before an armed Marine.

"Don't try to tell me what to do," she warned. "Just because there's a child between us does *not* give you rights over my life."

Chase's shoulders drooped and he knelt beside the couch, looking her in the eye. "I deal with people like that woman all the time." Her expression was doubtful. "I can't tell you how many of my customers have decided what they wanted only to insist my crew rip it out and start over a week later." When he realized she wasn't buying the comparison, he tried another route. "You're tired, Tessa. Your feet are swollen."

She looked at them, wiggling plump toes. "I've learned to live with it."

Chase sighed and snatched up a pillow, stuffing it beneath her knees, then pushing her back into the cushions. "I'm not trying to take over. God knows, I don't know squat about women's clothes." He flashed her that devastating grin. "Except maybe taking them off." Her eyes flared. *"But,"* he warned, "you're pushing yourself too hard." She opened her mouth and he put up his hand. "I swear I won't let that old biddy leave without buying at least one of your creations."

"She usually buys two, with shoes."

Chase smiled, the corners of his eyes crinkling, and Tessa felt the warmth of his honest feelings down to her sore feet. How had he wiggled his way into playing concerned lover? No, he wasn't after her, she reminded herself, but his child, and she refused to believe he was interested in her, the woman. His marriage proposal was a path into her baby's life. The baby obviously meant more to him than she had first imagined. Suddenly, Tessa hated him for trying to get close and she hated herself for getting comfortable.

Chase's lips thinned as her expression suddenly hardened. He didn't think someone so soft and lovely could deal such a loathsome look with that much power. He sighed tiredly, took the glass and set it on the desk.

"Rest, Miss Lightfoot," he said tersely, then moved to the door.

"Chase?"

He stilled, his hand on the knob, his back to her. "Yeah?"

"This doesn't change anything."

He glanced back over his shoulder, looking her over. "If you say so."

Tessa did not like the sound of that.

Not at all.

"He actually came in here and sold dresses?" Dia said when she arrived twenty minutes after Chase had left, and Tessa wanted to pinch her. It wasn't that big a deal. Yet when Dana nodded, Dia squealed with laughter. Tessa gave her sister a thin-lidded glare, and Dana, impressionable creature that she was, gushed.

"He's so cute and Miss Dewberry was just drooling over him. She bought the dresses you tried to get her to try on," Dana said to Tessa. "You know, the ones that actually *fit*." The salesgirl turned back to Dia. "He even sold her shoes and a hat! God—" Dana fanned herself, sighing dreamily "—he fills out those jeans *sooo* nicely. For a man his age, of course."

"Of course," Dia agreed, her smile quivering.

Dana looked at Tessa suddenly. "How do you know him?"

Tessa's skin fused with heat and she glanced at Dia. "He's ah—um—" How was she supposed to explain this? It was all getting so complicated. She looked at Dia, her expression pleading for help.

Dia let her squirm for a few seconds, then said, "He's just a friend...of the family, you could say."

Dana nodded, obviously satisfied, and excused herself to collect the remnants of Chase's whirlwind sales victory.

"Where is he now?"

"How the hell should I know!"

Dia reared back, eyeing her sister thoughtfully. "God, you are tired."

"No, I'm not." Tessa flipped through hung garments,

checking the sizes. "I'm angry. You were no help in that meeting yesterday, Dia. None."

Dia's brows drew down and she pulled Tessa from the center of the store and into the little alcove behind the register. She gripped her sister's arms, forcing her to calm down.

"Whether you think that or not is irrelevant. Chase Madison could have sued for custody, Tessa. He still could." Tessa paled. "We're damn lucky he has a heart, because if he didn't, as soon as you gave birth, this baby could have been taken by the courts until an agreement was reached. Do you want someone else holding your newborn baby before you? Caring for her? Deciding your child's future? Or would it kill you to be his friend?"

"Yes. It will," Tessa cried dejectedly, the images her sister painted striking her hard. "It will give him leverage. I can't trust him."

Dia let her go and stepped back. "No one says you have to marry the man, for God's sake."

"No one but him."

"Oh, get real." Tessa arched a brow and Dia's features stretched taut as she said, "You're serious?"

"Don't listen to the messages on your private line much, do you? I called you immediately after our lunch, all night and this morning."

Dia's gazed faltered. "I was...out of town for the evening."

Tessa gave her sister the once-over, then smiled softly. At least someone was having fun, she thought, then explained their lunch date.

Dia folded her arms and propped her hip against the counter, looking very much the high-powered attorney. "Did he badger you?"

Arranging ribbons on a dowel rod, Tessa gave her a side glance. "No."

"Would you consider his visit harassment?"

"No." How could she? He'd helped her, saw that her best customer was satisfied, and had only her best health in mind, damn him. If he hadn't forced her to rest, she'd have kept going and that wouldn't have been good for her *or* her baby.

"If we put a restraining order on him, it might make him pursue custody."

"Then don't." Tessa dropped her head back onto her shoulders, sighing long and slow. "I'm not due for another three months—let's not look for trouble. Maybe he'll lose interest."

When Dia didn't respond, Tessa looked at her sister. "Don't hold your breath," she finally said.

Tessa felt as if she were tottering on a peg with nothing to stop her fall, waiting for the shove that would send her into oblivion. "Go ahead, say it, I see it in your eyes."

"I've never seen a man more determined to be a father, Tessa."

"Me, either," came dispiritedly.

Dia laid a hand on her arm, forcing Tessa to meet her gaze and listen hard. "Then perhaps for once in your life you ought to quit planning out every facet with annoyingly meticulous detail and just go with it."

Tessa eyed her warily. "You like him, don't you?"

Dia shrugged elegantly clad shoulders. "I'm not the one who matters, but yes. He's charming, handsome, smart, a decorated ex-Marine, owns his own business, comes from a good family." Her eyes sparkled suddenly, devilishly. "Has two drop-dead gorgeous brothers—"

"Great." She rolled her eyes. "If he's won you over, what chance have I got? And isn't that conflict of interest or something?"

"Hey, I wouldn't worry so much, Sis," Dia said, slinging her arm over her sister's shoulder and dropping a kiss to her temple. "He hasn't met Mom or Samantha. They'll make any man run for the hills."

Tessa laughed softly at the picture of her eccentric mother and Chase in the same room. Even though she never wanted him *that* deep into her life, it would be something to see. She wondered idly what he'd say if her mother read his palm before ever speaking to him.

The door chime jingled and Tessa said goodbye to her sister. Dia flipped open her cellular phone, thumb-dialed a call as she grabbed her briefcase and left the shop in a brisk walk. Dia needed to slow down, Tessa thought. She was always in a rush to be somewhere she wasn't.

Tessa walked over to the customer, smiling and offering herb tea. The older, distinguished-looking woman smiled back, so warm and endearingly gentle that Tessa felt the tension in her wash away like a summer rain. This was the first person in a long time to look at her and not her tummy. As Tessa went to prepare tea, she decided that Chase Madison could be as charming and as likable as he wanted. Her guard was up, cemented into place, and ex-Marine or not, he wasn't storming past it.

Chase's gaze snapped up from the pile of tomatoes so carefully arranged in the bin. "Are you following me?" he asked hopefully.

"Hardly." Tessa's eyes narrowed on him, her hand on her hip. "I could ask the same of you."

"Yes." Unashamed, reckless.

"What?"

"I found out you shopped here, every Monday morning, at nine." His forehead wrinkled a bit. "Are you always so predictable?"

"No." She jammed tomatoes into a plastic sack.

"Careful, they'll bruise."

"I want to bruise you," she hissed over the stack of red fruits.

Chase's grin widened.

"Will you quit smiling!"

He didn't. "Bothers you, doesn't it?"

"Everything about you bothers me." She dropped her selection into the cart and moved on.

Chase rounded the bin and dogged her heels. "What

bothers you the most? That I'm the father of our baby or that you're attracted to me?''

"Is your ego always so overblown, Mr. Madison?''

He caught the cart, keeping her near, and Tessa felt her insides shift and twist. And it had nothing, absolutely *nothing* to do with her baby. Those disgustingly sculptured shoulders of his looked bigger and more muscular than when he was in her shop on Saturday, his eyes a darker blue and unspeakably intimate as they traveled the line of her body, caressing it without touching. As if they weren't in the middle of the produce aisle drawing attention, for heaven's sake.

"Admit it, you feel this—'' he inhaled through clenched teeth, his gaze simmering ''—this assault on the senses, the blood, every time we get close.''

"Sexual attraction is hardly the basis for a relationship—'' Oh, what made her admit that?

"Aha. So you have thought about it.''

He was grinning again, the rat. "No.'' Her reddening cheeks contradicted her.

"Liar.''

"I'm not lying. Now, leave me alone.'' She brushed him aside with the cart. He was right beside her, nodding to the eavesdroppers and interested customers.

"I'm here, Tessa, to stay. Get used to it.'' Half threat, half coaxing.

"Not a chance.'' She wouldn't look at him, dropping item after item into her cart.

Chase knew he was getting to her. "God, you eat that?''

She looked to see what he meant and frowned, then snatched up the sardines, replaced them on the shelf and reached for tuna. Oh, just go away, she thought.

"Got you all confused, don't I? Wondering where I'll turn up next?''

She spared him a withering glance. "Amuse yourself with the idea, Mr. Madison. You have so far.''

"I'm going to do more than amuse myself with it,'' he said with a long glance down her body. Those eyes were

dangerous, she thought, and was about to ask him what he
had planned in the let's-mess-up-Tessa's-life scenario,
when someone called out.

"Hey boss, you're needed on the site!"

Chase twisted, nodding to a man dressed in work clothes,
a tool belt slung over his shoulder, a cellular phone in his
hand.

Chase looked back at Tessa, loving her wide, puzzled
eyes. He had her flustered nicely, he thought, and let im-
pulse take him. He wrapped his arm around her, pulling
her flush against him. His child kicked, as if joining its
mother's effort as she pushed at his chest.

"Let go." She glanced around nervously, then looked at
him, embarrassment blooming in her face.

He bent, inhaling the scent of cinnamon near her ear, and
whispered, "I can't. I've never walked away from a challenge." His words burned her skin, sending gooseflesh
down her throat to her breasts. "And baby or not, Tessa
Lightfoot—" Her fingers flexed on his chest and she closed
her eyes. "It's *you* I want."

Even though she would never believe him, his words
sank into her heart like tiny arrows, weakening her resolve.
She pushed at his chest. "No, Chase, you can't," she whispered back, then gasped as his lips ground against her neck
in a hot, quick kiss before he pulled away.

They stared at each other for an instant and Tessa
touched her throat, feeling warm and tingly all over. That
was…was…delicious.

He smiled slowly, privately. Then he left her standing in
the middle of the aisle between the cabbages and kumquats.
Gripping the cart, Tessa watched him, his broad back, his
indecently tight behind. Her heart pounding in her throat,
her body awake and alive with sweet, quick passion. It had
been so long she almost didn't recognize the sensation. Not
that it had ever been like *that*. And she wondered, hoped,
she had at least *some* effect on him.

When he met up with his crewman and back-stepped to
look at her, Tessa's gaze dropped briefly to the well-worn

mold of his jeans. She smiled, smug as realization played across his face. His skin darkened, his expression sheepish as he shoved his hands into his pockets.

She wasn't without a little power.

And it made them even.

Later that evening, Carole Anne Madison shifted to the edge of the Queen Anne tapestry settee, her hands poised on her lap as she stared up at her eldest son. Chase saw her gaze flick to his father, the pipe clenched in his teeth. Idly, Chase wondered if it was lit this time.

"She's a lovely woman, Chase."

"You saw her!" Chase's wide eyes narrowed suddenly. "She didn't know it was you, did she? God, Mom, if she thinks we're all ganging up on her, she might leave town!" He paced, wearing a path in the carpet. The last thing he wanted was to scare Tessa.

"Chase dearest, please."

"You're mother isn't an imbecile, Chase, don't treat her like one."

"Carl, hush. He's just concerned, as we all are." She patted the space beside her, and Chase paced a bit more, then sank down beside her, rubbing his hand over his face.

"I like her, Chase. She's poised, gracious. One can tell a great deal about a person when you're in their territory."

Though those were not the traits Tessa had shown him, Chase took his mother's word for it. "And you discovered?"

Carole Anne looked thoughtful before she spoke. "She makes everyone feel welcome, instantly. Even offered tea and joined me to have it. She's very honest about her designs and whom they suit." His mother paused, her eyes unusually bright. "And your baby's growing beautifully." Chase enjoyed the happiness spreading across his mother's face.

His father cleared his throat. "It's just like you to do everything backwards, boy."

Chase stiffened and left his chair in a lurch, wondering

if his father would ever forgive him for not becoming a politician. As usual, his mother defended him with a sharp glare at his dad.

"Do you think Janis did this thing with the computer mix-up?" his mother asked.

Chase shrugged. "I wouldn't put it past her." He didn't want to address his suspicions, not when Tessa could use them to keep him out of his child's life. Things were just too fragile right now. "But then we all know how she hated being excommunicated from the Madison clan." The divorce settlement had nearly made Chase broke, and he eyed his father, all too aware that the man had never liked Janis, thought she was a gold digger, and had let him know it on a regular basis. Yet Chase had understood her need to feel part of a family. Of course, only Senator Madison's family would do. His dad thought Janis had married him because of who his father was, and finally, Chase had been inclined to believe it.

"Oh, Chase," his mother said suddenly. "But this is so wonderful." He gazed at her and saw tears, tears she never shed in front of anyone. He sank to one knee in front of her. "I hoped that you or your brothers would find women to love like I love your father." Beyond them, Carl Madison softened, in expression and posture, and he came to his wife, settling beside her and enfolding her hand in his.

"I'm not in love with Tessa Lightfoot, Mom." In *lust* would be a better word. He couldn't believe how turned on he was by this particular woman, pregnant or not. "And I can truthfully say she wishes I was never born."

Carole Anne's brow wrinkled softly. "She really is obstinate about your involvement?"

"She wants me gone. Trust me."

Carole Anne smiled slightly. "But you like her."

The corner of Chase's mouth quirked. "Oh yes."

"That's all I needed to hear," she said succinctly. "We'll stand back and promise not to interfere. At all." His mother looked pointedly at his father. "*Won't we*, Carl?" Though there was a softness in her voice, her sharp blue eyes warned his father there would be hell to pay if he so much as spoke to Tessa without Chase's permission. His father finally nodded and Chase leaned forward, kissed her forehead and whispered, ''I knew I could count on you, Mom. Thanks.''

He left, glad his parents weren't going to stick their noses into this. Chase wanted his baby in the worst way. But after spending several sleepless nights with Tessa Lightfoot's image bursting across his mind, Chase wanted more. He wanted to see if he wasn't fooling himself about this energy they shared, the way she could stir his senses into madness. He wanted to kiss her, *really* kiss her. But as he thought of her perfectly lush mouth, a mouth made for old-fashioned slow, wet kisses, Chase figured at this point, she'd just bite him.

Four

In her doctor's office two days later, Tessa looked up from the magazine and frowned. The hint of a voice, a *male* voice, pricked her attention and she strained to define it. When the receptionist called her name, she rushed past the partition and froze.

Chase. His shoulder propped against the wall, he was obviously receiving a thorough explanation of the birth process, via a wall diagram, from the pretty blond nurse. Tessa didn't like that he was here, didn't like that he'd used that oozing Madison charm to worm his way past the front desk of a women's clinic, and she did not like the way Blondie was looking at him as if he could cure cancer.

Oh, you're really keeping those emotions under control, aren't you? She cleared her throat and something inside her leapt—she swore it was indigestion—when he dismissed the young nurse without a glance and came to her.

"*What* are you doing *here?*" she asked the instant he was near.

"I saw the appointment on your calendar when I was at

the store on Saturday," he said absently as he sketched her quickly from head to toe. "God, you look beautiful, Tessa."

She couldn't help the flutter in her chest, and unconsciously smoothed her vest and slacks. Then she shook her head, dismissing his compliments and focusing her attention on why he was here. To invade her privacy, her life. To take her baby.

I'm not visiting my child, he'd said. *I want him.* It terrified her to think just how determined Chase Madison could be.

"*Mr.* Madison," finally came through tightly clenched teeth.

Chase sighed dispiritedly. She was upset. Well, he didn't expect her not to be. But after his great sales job the other day, he'd hoped she'd be just a little glad to see him. Tessa was a hard nut to crack; this wall she built around herself, for his benefit he knew, was like coming up against ice. For a time she thawed, then something triggered the quick freeze job and Chase found himself back at the beginning. But he wasn't giving up.

"You can't be here." She glanced around at the personnel and patients listening.

"I'm the father, Tessa. I have the right."

"No, you don't. It's my body."

"Your body's nurturing *my* baby."

"Yours?" a feminine voice asked.

They turned and Chase found a statuesque older woman wearing green hospital scrubs. *Faraday* was stenciled across the pocket.

"Tessa?" She frowned between the two. "Who is this?"

Tessa cast Chase a superior glance and said, "Test tube number 3–4–6 dash whatever," then ignored him and his narrowing look as she looped her arm with Dr. Johanna Faraday's, drawing her away and whispering quickly. Dr. Faraday spoke calmly, glancing intermittently at Chase.

"Well, at least he doesn't have the warts and baldness you wanted."

"What he has is the ability to charm the socks off your staff, my sister and my employees. He shouldn't even be here."

"Calm down, Tessa. And you're right. An ob/gyn clinic isn't the usual male stomping grounds, but the test proved he *is* 346-1010, and that gives him the same rights as any other father. Especially since he didn't sign them away."

"No, he didn't." She had to admit that. He was a victim of a computer foul-up as much as she was. But that didn't change the fact that Chase was here, trying to wiggle into her appointment like he was...what? The father? Concerned about her? Hah.

Johanna tapped her pen against her lips, then tucked it behind her ear. "You've acknowledged him as the father?"

"As the *donor*." She couldn't think of him as anything else. She just couldn't. Where Chase and his rights were concerned, she *had* to keep her emotions out of it.

Johanna looked thoughtful, then sighed with that I've-come-to-a-decision look. "He doesn't have the right to accompany you in the exam, but in all honesty I can't make him leave. Fathers have rights." Johanna leaned a touch closer. "Is he going to give you trouble, get violent?"

Tessa cast him a quick glance. Chase? Violent? She didn't know him well enough to make that judgment. But the man smiled more than a kid at Christmas. "I doubt it."

Tessa felt as if she were losing control of the situation the minute Johanna Faraday motioned to Chase, then indicated her office. She sent Tessa a *behave* glance before they disappeared inside. Tessa sat, then Johanna addressed the man standing behind the extra chair.

"I must think of the welfare of my patient first, Mr. Madison, and Miss Lightfoot does not want you here."

Her patient, Chase noticed, wouldn't look at him. Instead she twisted the silken cord of her purse into a hangman's noose. "Miss Lightfoot would rather I vanish off the face of the earth," he said with a half smile and a glance in her direction. "But I'm not."

"Why *did* you come here, Mr. Madison?"

He felt Tessa's gaze on him, but looked at the doctor. "Because my baby is growing inside her and I have the right to know how well." He glanced at Tessa.

Something flickered in her eyes, so brief Chase almost didn't catch it. He wished he knew her well enough to decipher it. "She's supposed to have a sonogram today. I want to know if everything is okay, with Tessa and my child."

"For a man who offered no more than a few ounces of fluid, you're asking for a lot." Tessa glared up at him, hating that he looked so good, hating that he was being so reasonable. He didn't give a hoot about her, just this baby and his, however small, part in its creation.

The fractured anger and fear in her words struck him hard, with insight and just enough frustration to want to shake her. "Yes, I didn't have any part in this, and yes, I wasn't consulted, but there is more than our feelings and rights at stake now. There is the child. Our child," he gestured between himself and Tessa and out of the corner of his eye saw her shoulders stiffen. "And whether you like it or not," he said, turning his gaze to Tessa and meeting her stare, "that infant—" he nodded to her tummy "—needs everyone who cares about him, protecting him and his rights." God, Chase thought, he loved this baby already. He lowered his voice, speaking to Tessa as if they didn't have an audience. "Think what you want, Tessa, but I didn't come here to upset you. After what happened in the Golden Dragon, I realized how unbelievably miraculous this all is."

Tessa felt a lump work in her throat, at the raw emotion playing across his features, lacing his voice with a tender roughness.

"And I only wanted some of the experiences I've already missed." He held her gaze a moment longer, then looked at Dr. Faraday. "Take good care of her," he said, then left without a word.

Both women stared at the empty doorway, then at each other.

Tessa's eyes burned and she felt awful. "Oh hell, now what do I do?"

"He could stand beyond the curtain and listen."

Tessa stared at her lap. This was so personal. And they hadn't even really kissed, for heaven's sake. But the look in his eyes, oh God, she felt as if she were cheating him. She *was* cheating him. Finally Tessa nodded and Johanna left the office to catch him. Outside the door she heard Johanna laying down the rules. She didn't even look at him. God, she was being a coward, but every minute with the man had her feeling like a general losing ground in a battle. Still, the excitement in his voice hurt. Only the baby, she reminded herself. He wants this only for the baby.

The sonogram was under way when Tessa heard a nurse escort him in through the hall door. She glanced down and saw his shoes beneath the curtain, but even with Johanna talking louder than usual, he didn't utter a word, didn't move.

Then Chase heard the rapid, steady heartbeat. His breath caught in his chest, a violent surge of air that left him stunned. *Alive.* Alive, his brain shouted. His child. Flesh and bone and blood were growing, breathing in there, waiting to be born. Waiting to be loved and protected. And he rejoiced in the warm feeling racing through his body, pushing his pulse to match his child's.

Then suddenly the heartbeat stopped.

"What happened?" Panic filled his voice.

Johanna's was calm. "I just moved to a different area, Mr. Madison, wait. Listen? There it is again. Oh look, Tessa, her fingers."

Abruptly, Chase whipped the curtain back and stared first at Tessa, her belly so round and smooth and covered with some slimy gel, then beyond her to the monitor. And Chase saw a tiny fist unfurl. His eyes burned and he leaned closer, scanning every detail.

"Do you mind?" Tessa said, but he wasn't listening. He was awed. There was no other word for it. And Tessa thought right there that things could have been worse. He could have been like Ryan, who hoped never to see this sight. But Chase Madison was looking at her now as if she could spin straw into gold.

Dr. Faraday and she exchanged a glance, Johanna's gaze dropping to the black-and-white printout. She tore it off and offered it to him. Hesitantly, he accepted it, his eyes searching the undefinable shades of gray for the unborn life hidden within. The doctor peered over the sheet and pointed. And Tessa realized that strong, handsome, ex-Marine, construction engineer Chase Madison was very close to tears. The sight left her stunned. He gazed down at her, then he bent and kissed her, quick and hard on the mouth.

Then he left.

And Tessa, though oddly delighted to see a man brought to his knees by the sight of an unborn child, realized just how much he wanted to be her baby's father. And exactly how much *she* didn't matter.

Tigh McBain raced forward and slammed the ball against the court wall, believing he had his racquetball partner in the clinch. But Chase dived out, sneakers squeaking as he skidded to a halt and smashed the tiny ball to the baseline. Tigh knew he'd never get the return in time and tossed the racquet to the floor.

"I give." Bent over, breathing heavily, he braced his hands on his thighs before he fell flat on his face.

"You?" Chase tugged the tank top from his shorts and swiped the sweat from his face with the hem.

"Yes, me," came back tightly. "God, where do you get the energy?"

Chase thought about Tessa and smiled to himself. "I don't sit behind a desk getting fat."

Tigh straightened immediately, scowling, and Chase noticed he couldn't resist touching his stomach. Chase laughed.

"Come on, I'll buy you one of those energy shakes."

"I'd rather have a beer."

"That's your problem," Chase told him. "Besides, it's not even 10 a.m."

"You can really be a sanctimonious pain sometimes, you know," Tigh said as they left the court. Chase drained a bottle of water without stopping, then slung his gym bag over his shoulder and headed out to the car. Tigh was a little slower, stopping to flirt with a pretty woman whose only job was to hand out towels. She was helping him use one, Chase decided.

"That's jailbait," Chase said as Tigh caught up to him.

"Nah, she's twenty."

"And you're thirty."

Tigh looked at Chase and frowned, his features going slack as if he had just realized how old he was. He glanced back at the girl, smiled, then faced forward as they walked to the car.

"You were in Tessa's doctor's office yesterday morning," Tigh said suddenly as Chase unlocked his car door.

Oblivious to the censure in Tigh's tone, Chase's face split into a smile. "It was incredible, Tigh, to actually see my baby moving around inside her. My heart was beating so fast I thought I'd pass out."

Both men slid into the Jeep and buckled up. "You shouldn't invade her privacy like that, Chase. She could put a restraining order on you. It's damn close to stalking."

Chase scowled as he pulled into traffic. "My intentions are very clear. And she knows it."

Tigh eyed his client. "Is there something I should know about you and Miss Lightfoot? I don't want her sister slapping you with a lawsuit that I know nothing about."

"Dia would, wouldn't she?"

"Hell, yeah. She's a criminal lawyer first, pal. Everything to her is a fight to the last drop of blood, guilty or innocent."

Chase stared at the windshield. "She seemed so reserved."

"*Reserved* and a *circling shark* are often confused. Now, answer the question."

"I can't say, because there's nothing to tell."

"Bull."

"Tessa doesn't want to see this go to court and neither do I. We have our child's best interests to think about. So far, she tolerates me and I lust after her."

"You're kidding."

It was such a bland delivery that Chase glanced at Tigh as he pulled to a halt. "Crazy, huh?" He shut off the engine and left the car.

Tigh leaned over the gearshift and groaned. "For God's sake! Why do you pay me for legal advice, then go and do this?" He gestured to Tessa's Attic.

Chase leaned into the car window. "Because you're my kid brother's best friend and I used to protect you from bullies."

Tigh flushed red at the memory. "That smacks of tremendous confidence in my abilities, Chase. And I advise you to back off from her."

"Not a chance." Chase gestured for Tigh to join him but Tigh waved him off, sagging into the car seat. Chase straightened and headed through the door. Someone whistled softly and he looked up to see Dana leaning out over the counter, her gaze running the length of his legs.

"Not bad, Mr. Madison."

Somehow the compliment was lost with the *mister* tacked on. "Is she here?"

Dana inclined her head toward the rear of the store just as Chase heard a crash and a soft yelp of pain. He was in the back office in a heartbeat.

A blind was hanging precariously off the window frame as Tessa rubbed the top of her head. He strode to her, catching her by the arms.

"Are you all right?"

Tessa took one look at him in his shorts with brown muscles rippling everywhere and it set her teeth on edge. "Yes, dammit." She shifted out of his grip, touching her scalp and inspecting her fingers for blood. "I'm fine, *the baby's fine* and what are you doing here, again?"

He pulled the stepladder closer to the window and climbed up to reattach the blind. "I just came by to say hi."

Mentally, Tessa groaned. His taut behind was at eye level. This wasn't fair. Yet as much as he annoyed her by busting in, unannounced, the totally female side of her said, step back and inspect the hardware. She did. He had great legs and damned if he didn't look sexy, even sweaty, his hair sopping wet, his tank top marked with dampness. And those skimpy running shorts with side slits, good God, they clung. "Do I look like I have time to chat, or don't you work for a living anymore?" She managed to pull her gaze to a decent level when he hopped off the stepladder.

"Sure—" he leaned down in her face, smiling. "But I take time away, so I don't mutate into a psycho."

"I'm not—oh, never mind." It was useless to argue with him when he was grinning like that. She moved around to her desk and scanned invoices, not really seeing them.

"You need to relax."

"You need to leave." She didn't bother looking up.

"Gee. If I knew you better I'd say you weren't happy to see me."

She delivered a scathing glance. "What gave you that idea?" came dryly.

Chase frowned. She looked pale. "Have you eaten breakfast yet?"

"I'll remind you to mind your own business and not to tell me what to do, Mr. Madison."

So, they were back to that again. "You need to—"

"I need? I need!" She tossed the invoices on the desk. "What the hell do you know about what I *need*?"

Stunned by her temper, he grasped her arms with a gentle hold, forcing her to look him in the eye. "I'd like to know, Tessa."

"Nothing from you."

"You're going to get it."

She frowned, eyeing him thoroughly. "That sounds too much like a threat."

He grinned, briefly kissing her forehead. "I'm not out to hurt you, Tessa. One of these days you'll have to trust me on it."

"I have no reason to trust you."

"You will." Chuckling, he moved away, heading to the door. "You will."

Tessa's gaze dropped to his behind shifting beneath the silky nylon shorts. She didn't trust *herself*, not when she wanted to reach out and squeeze that behind.

Christian Madison braced his shoulder against the window frame and watched the delivery truck pull up before his brother's offices. He shook his head before twisting a look at Chase, elbow deep in paperwork. "She sent them back. Again."

Chase looked up and grinned. "I expected as much." Especially after the dismissal in her shop yesterday.

Christian rolled around and folded his arms over his stomach. His gaze flicked to Colin, who lounged in a leather chair beside Chase's desk. "How long are you going to keep this up? Till you're in debt over shipping costs?"

"As long as it takes," Chase said, leaving his desk and heading for the door.

"Can't you see she doesn't want anything from you, Bro?" Colin called to his big brother but Chase was already out of sight.

Chase met the deliveryman in the office foyer, his staff tuned to their conversation. He tipped the guy extra to make the return trip and put a smile back on his face. Stubborn woman. They were only gifts for their child.

Tessa folded her arms over her tummy and gave the deliveryman a dirty look before he made it to the first porch step.

"Take them back."

His muscular shoulders drooped. "Ma'am, these are the same packages you sent back yesterday *and* this morning."

Tessa stared at the crate for a moment, then stepped back from the open door and motioned him inside. He gestured to his partner, and within minutes the corner of her living room was filled with packages from the finest stores in the city.

Dammit, Chase. They'd been at this since early yesterday afternoon, and the man just wouldn't get the message. Closing the door, she moved to the phone and dialed her sister. She got the answering machine. She started to tell her lawyer to take out a restraining order on him, then thought better of it and hung up without speaking. She glared at the five-foot-high stack of boxes. She wasn't going to open a single one. But she wasn't going to spend her one day off venting her anger on the deliverymen either.

"Hey, lady, you can't park there!"

"I just did," Tessa said, walking determinedly up the slope. She stopped in front of him and as the breeze molded the billowy jean dress to her body, his gaze immediately dropped to her belly. "Chase Madison. Where is he?"

He swallowed first. "Now you just stand right here, ma'am, and I'll find him. Don't move, okay." He put up his hands as if to keep her there, and Tessa offered him a sweet smile. Pregnant women had that effect on some men. It was an advantage she seized.

"Find him, quickly," she said a little breathlessly, and dramatically touched her stomach. He took off like a shot, leaping stacks of lumber and equipment. It did nothing to lighten her mood. She was still going to get Daddy Warbucks to back off and out of her life, starting now.

"Hey boss, got a visitor," Dave called to Chase a few minutes later.

Chase waved him back as he finished testing the concrete mix, then stood and motioned for his crew to start pouring.

"Inspectors?"

"Not a chance."

Chase turned at his foreman's tone and frowned. Dave was glancing back over his shoulder nervously. It was the first time he'd seen his former Marine gunnery sergeant unsure. Chase stepped over iron framework and climbed out of the hole. He saw Tessa immediately, watched her brush loose strands of black hair from her cheek. Quickly he strode to a bucket of water to wash the sweat and dirt from his face and arms. He kept watching her as he dried himself, then advanced, tossing the towel to Dave.

"You get that girl pregnant, boss?"

"Hey, Dave, you know me."

Dave smirked at the innocent look. "Yeah, that's why I asked."

"Button it up! Lady on the lot!" Chase shouted, and his crew threw on shirts and knew to keep their language clean. He moved down the small slope to meet her.

Tessa watched him come, a relaxed long-legged stride that made her pulse leap. Even with his jeans and T-shirt covered with gray gunk, he looked sexy. It really was unfair! To make matters worse, he stopped a little too close for comfort.

She took a step back and shielded her eyes to look up at him. "This has to stop, Mr. Madison."

"When are you going to call me Chase?" After the doctor's office, he'd hoped they'd gone past that.

"When pigs fly."

"They do."

"What?"

"In planes."

She sent him a disgusted look.

"Swine of indeterminate variety have been known to board aircraft and fly."

Her lips twitched. Well, heck. How was she supposed to argue with that kind of logic? "Chase," she said tiredly, and he grinned at the victory. "The gifts have to stop."

"I want my son to have the best."

"*I* can provide for *my* child."

"But Dana said you hadn't bought anything yet."

"Interrogating my employees while I was incapacitated. Great," she muttered, glancing away.

"She was just making conversation. Don't blame Dana. I thought I could help out a little."

Her gaze snapped back to his. "Can't you get it through your head? I don't want you in my life. I don't want anything from you!" She was shouting, her fist clenched.

And Chase reared back. "Good God,Tessa. Calm down."

Her gaze thinned. "I *am* calm." Her lips scarcely moved.

"No, you're not," he said. "And standing in the sun isn't helping. Come on." Whether she liked it or not, he took her arm and escorted her to where his car was parked beneath the shade of a tree. She was grateful for the reprieve. She looked at the black Jeep Grand Cherokee, then to her maroon one.

He smirked. "It seems we have similar tastes, at least."

Same make, same year. It was creepy.

"Want some water?"

"Yes," she said, just to gather her thoughts. He moved to the rear of the Jeep and poked around in a cooler. Tessa stole a moment to peek inside the vehicle, hoping to get an idea about this man. On the seat was a cellular phone, a portable fax, and papers filling an accordion file, but that was the only neat spot she could see. The rest of the Jeep was littered with rolled-up clothes, muddy boots, paper cups and a hundred fast-food wrappers. He lives out of this thing, she thought as he came back with two bottles of water. He cracked the seal and handed her one.

Chase watched her, his favorite pastime lately, as she drank.

"Now tell me the real reason you won't accept my gifts. It's my child, too."

"Yes. This is your baby." He smiled hugely. "*But* I was artificially inseminated, Chase, by number 3–4–6 dash something or other, and that's what I think of you." His expression withered quickly, sadly, and the sight of it sent a shaft of pain through her chest. "I did this because I wanted a child, my *own* child. Not with the hope that the father would butt his nose in and ruin my plans.''

Chase felt something clench at his chest, taking his breath, and he stared off into the distance and swallowed hard. ''I can't *not want* this, Tessa. So don't ask. I never thought I'd get this chance.'' He met her gaze. ''And how can a few gifts ruin anything?''

''A few? For heaven's sake, did you buy Bloomingdale's or just the infant department?''

His smile was a little strained. ''It was too much fun. Just thinking about this baby makes me crazy.''

''You can't do this, Chase.'' Her voice wavered. ''No furniture or clothes, not yet, not again.''

Again? He searched her features, the tightness around her mouth bearing a tension that spoke volumes. ''Tell me what's got you so scared?''

She sighed against the Jeep, drank water, then looked at him. ''I've lost a child before, Chase.'' The color drained from his face. ''And it was hard. Very hard.'' Her throat closed up and she drank more water, staring anywhere but at him. ''I bought everything and then when I miscarried, it hurt just to look at it all.'' It hurt to remember Ryan's insensitivity, to remember she failed at everything but her work. ''I gave it to charity and swore I wouldn't buy a thing—'' she met his gaze ''—till I held my child in my arms.''

The tears in her eyes hit him like a punch to the gut and Chase tossed his empty bottle into his Jeep as he stepped closer. He made to hold her, then let his arms fall to his sides. ''I'm sorry, Tessa.'' He drove his fingers through his hair. ''God, I can be such an idiot sometimes.'' She shrugged, and he scoffed, half amused. ''Agreeing on something, are we?''

''I suppose.'' Humor lit her eyes.

But his uneasiness wouldn't leave. ''How far along were you when you miscarried?''

''Twelve weeks.'' The words came slowly and warily.

''What does Dr. Faraday say about this baby?''

She looked suddenly affronted. "Mind your own business, Chase."

He leaned close, in her face. "You *are* my business, Tessa." He braced his hands on the Jeep, on either side of her head, hemming her in. "You aren't going to lose this child," he said with absolute conviction. "He's got Madison blood in him. And if I have to watch you every second of the day, I will."

Great. Now she'd turned him into a bloodhound-slash-nanny. "Look. I'm not stupid, Chase. I'm very careful. And I got this far—" she gestured to her belly with both hands "—without you."

He pressed softly against her, hearing her breath catch and loving the feel of her tummy between them. For a moment he simply stared into her belligerent green eyes, then, like a falcon to his prey, he swooped down and covered her mouth with his.

Tessa jolted, dropping the water bottle and pushing at his chest. She turned her head to avoid him, but he followed her mouth, tasting her over and over. And then she let him. He held her motionless without the touch of his hands, his lips and tongue rolling lushly over hers, driving ripple after ripple of hot excitement through her body. Her mind screamed to hit him, gore him, but she couldn't. It felt like centuries since she'd been kissed and never like this. Oh God, *never.* Her legs felt weightless, and he kissed her. Moans escaped her throat and still he kissed her, and kissed her, until she wasn't pushing him away, but gripping his shirt by the fistfuls. She wanted more and when he slid his tongue over her lips, she opened for him, deepening their kiss, exploring the flavor of him and letting the sensual pull of this man take her somewhere new. *Ohh, Chase.*

Chase felt the moment she gave in, felt her soften deliciously, her breathing quicken with his. Her body rose to greet him and he wanted so much to hold her in his arms, but didn't dare. This was more incredible than he had imagined. He could do this forever, just stand here, loving her mouth. And when she opened for him, he thought he'd come apart and he struggled to control his need for more. *Yes, more.* His fingers flexed on the cool metal frame of the Jeep and he knew he was close to erupting, too close. Before he did something stupid, he drew slowly back, stealing a short, soft kiss.

Tessa opened her eyes, expecting to see smugness in his expression, yet found only breathtaking tenderness.

"You didn't make this baby by yourself, Tessa." He brushed a wisp of hair from her face, watching his movements before catching her gaze again. "And I might not have had the pleasure of being inside you first," he rasped near her ear, a shiver dancing down her body. "But a part of me is now."

He retreated suddenly, forcing her to lose her grip on his shirt. He looked down at the wrinkled fabric, then back to her. Instantly, she lowered her gaze. But the message was clear. There was more growing here than a child.

Abruptly, Tessa pushed away from his Jeep and headed to hers, taking a moment to catch her breath before starting the engine. She'd messed this up good, she thought, avoiding a look at him as she drove off the lot, pebbles and dirt spitting with her speed. She'd given him a piece of herself in that kiss. And she couldn't take it back.

Chase watched until the dust cloud dissipated, then sagged back against the Jeep. He closed his eyes, his hand trembling as he pushed his fingers through his hair. He blew out a long, slow breath. If the woman only knew how much power she had over him and used it, he'd be in trouble. Lord knew, he was deep in it now, his jeans so tight across his hips he thought he'd split the seams if he so much as moved.

He'd never wanted anything as much as he wanted this baby, wanted to be a dad.

But after experiencing her desire, he wanted Tessa more.

Five

Chase hooked his thumbs in his belt loops and stared up at Tessa. They were back to square one. He could tell by the cold way she addressed him from her front doorstep. It was as if nothing had passed between them, as if they had never shared a mind-boggling kiss just hours ago on Lot 404. "I understand how you feel about the packages, Tessa. I thought I'd get them out of your sight."

Tessa wiped the perspiration from her face and throat with a towel slung around her neck. "That isn't necessary, now."

"Yes, it is," he said, advancing, inviting himself in. Two men followed and she stepped back to hold the door.

Inside, Chase stopped short. When he'd seen the gray Victorian house, he'd expected ruffles and lace and feminine clutter like her shop. No place for a man. But the spacious, rustic interior of her house made him feel welcome, relaxed. He could almost see a dark-haired little boy skidding across the wide polished floor like a Surf Ninja. The image made him smile, the tension leaving his body.

Someone cleared their throat, and Chase turned. Tessa inclined her head to the two men standing in her foyer.

"These suspicious-looking creatures are my brothers, Christian and Colin." Chase slung an arm around both. "Guys? Tessa." They nodded. "Mind your manners." Chase gave his brothers a friendly pat, pushed between them and moved away.

Now she knew for certain that Chase had told his entire family about their situation. The two Madison brothers looked at her as if they'd never seen a pregnant woman before. And Tessa was no less than stunned when Christian and Colin came forward and kissed her on the cheek.

"Hey, Tessa," Christian said in a dark, smooth voice.

"You're prettier than he described," Colin added, wiggling his brows.

Obviously, Chase didn't have a monopoly on the Madison charm, she thought, greeting them politely. She had to admit Dia was right. They were gorgeous, drop-dead and all.

As she closed the front door, out of the corner of her eye she noticed Chase inspecting her home. Somehow it didn't bug her as much as she thought it should and she walked over to her treadmill to switch off the beeping pacer.

Chase was right behind her. "Tell me you aren't running on that," he demanded.

"You try walking with an extra twenty pounds around your waist," she scoffed, "much less running." She drained the bottle of water.

"Did your doctor—?"

"Please don't start," she warned tiredly. "Yes, she okayed it. I was running before I got pregnant, now I walk. Satisfied?" Her gaze drifted over his shoulder to his brothers, who looked a little embarrassed for their sibling. Good, they shouldn't have come. He shouldn't have told *anyone*.

"You run?" For some reason that shocked him.

"And what do you do for exercise?" She really hated that she sounded condescending.

"My job."

Without thinking she looked him over, the muscles beneath his tanned skin that resembled warm bronze. With the appraisal came the memory of their kiss. "Yeah, I guess so." Feminine approval tinted her voice and she instantly wished the comment back when he smiled, Cheshire cat pleased. Damn.

Ignoring his grin, she directed them into the living room, then sat on a stool near her design table, out of harm's way. The Madison brothers worked like an efficient team, and as she admired the continuous flex of muscle in her living room, she decided it did a girl good to watch men do grunt work once in a while. All three were roughly the same build, but Christian was slightly taller and broodingly quiet. Colin looked as if Irish blood flowed in his veins with his reddish brown hair and twinkling hazel eyes. But only Chase had that quick, disarming smile, she admitted as he hefted another box. It was his deadliest weapon in the charm department. He flashed it at her at every opportunity, in case she forgot.

It took a dozen trips by each man to clear the gifts, and though Christian and Colin moved rapidly with every intention of getting out of an uncomfortable situation, Chase stopped on each trip to say something to her. It started out with impersonal stuff about her house, her flower garden out front, then progressed to how much he enjoyed looking at her, how good she looked flushed and damp. He did too, she thought, watching perspiration trickle down his temple. She had the urge to swipe it away and instead kept her hands on her thighs. As they loaded the last box, Tessa offered them iced tea, and while Christian and Colin drained theirs in record time, Chase wasn't as fast. Before she knew it, Colin and Christian were gone and Chase stood in her living room, holding the empty glasses. Resigned to the man's making a pest of himself today, she nodded toward the kitchen.

"What will you do with it all?" she said as she flipped on a light and moved to the sink. He was there, bracing his hip on the counter edge, handing her glasses to load into the dishwasher.

"I'll store it until you hold our baby in your arms," he said, and she looked up sharply. Her eyes dampened instantly, her gaze sweeping his features, and he reached out, brushing the back of his knuckles across her cheek. "Tessa?" She didn't move.

"Thank you, Chase," came in a whisper.

"Anytime." He let his hand drop.

Hers shook slightly as she reached into a cupboard for fresh glasses, then she moved quickly away from him, masking her sudden nervousness with pouring more tea and pulling chilled fruit out of the fridge. She wished he wouldn't stand so close. It brought the memory of how well he kissed and the taste of him. And the wonderful, clean smell of him she found so incredibly…inviting. God. She had to try harder to ignore him. He only wanted her baby, and all his charm and sensitivity was to that end.

While she was busy arranging fruit on a platter, Chase looked around the spotless kitchen. Everything in its proper place, he thought, then mischievously peeked in a drawer. Neat, orderly. He glanced up to make certain she was occupied, then tried a cabinet. Cans in order of size, boxes, too. Christ, even her spices were alphabetized! Was his child going to grow up with his shorts starched and his face always clean? Hell, Chase had to hire a housekeeper just to find his bed.

"Are you always this fanatical?"

"Excuse me?" Her tone should have put him on guard.

It didn't and he charged ahead. "You're organized to the hilt here." He waved to encompass the house.

"It's my life, Chase. You don't have to live it."

"Well…" He folded his arms over his stomach, looking like big Chief Ha-ha, and said, "I'm not sure I want my kid growing up with the fear of getting his dirty shoes on the floor."

She eyed him suspiciously. "Are you trying to start something?"

His gaze moved leisurely over her, and he found the oversized T-shirt and tights attractive as hell. "You inviting something?" he said with a grin.

Tessa rolled her eyes. "You're pathetic, Chase."

He frowned. "'Cause I'm attracted to you?"

She arched a brow, doubt in her expression. "You're attracted to the mother of your child, that's all." She headed to the dining room with the platter, and he hated the resolution in her voice.

He caught her arm, pulling her close against his side. Warmth meshed and mingled between them. "That wasn't a momma I kissed yesterday." She opened her mouth to protest. "No. Don't tell me that was a mistake, Tessa, because besides this baby, that was the best thing to happen to me in a *long* time."

He stared at her with such blatant desire, she thought he was going to kiss her again. But instead he snatched a slice of fruit off the platter, popped it into his mouth, then strode to the door.

"See ya. I'm late for a ball game."

She blinked, feeling incredibly stupid. "Baseball?"

"Yup." He spun back to face her and made like he was hitting a ball, adding sound effects of the ball cracking against a bat, of the crowd cheering wildly, then he pulled a cap from his back pocket. He positioned it on his head and fairly bounced down her front steps.

It wasn't until she finished her fruit that she admitted she was actually...jealous of a baseball game.

Oh, God.

This was not good.

Two days later, Chase stared at the man over the desk and felt like a kid at the principal's office. The administrator looked over the papers containing his background and what he could find on Tessa's.

"You left the child's name and birth date blank."

"I know."

"I cannot submit an application to Trojan Academy, sir, without it."

Chase shifted uncomfortably in the chair. This is where it got a little sticky.

"He isn't born yet."

Thergoode peered over the rim of his glasses. "I beg your pardon?"

"Miss Lightfoot is pregnant with my child and I want him to attend this school. Since your waiting list is damn near three years, I figured it wouldn't hurt to get a head start."

"You understood incorrectly, sir."

Instantly Chase disliked Thergoode's superior look and knew this interview wasn't going to go well.

"Trojan Academy is the finest school in the county and, yes, we screen all applicants thoroughly. But not only is your child unborn, but he or she isn't even—" The round, pudgy man looked away for a moment and a rage of absolute proportions slithered through Chase.

"Legitimate?" came ground between clenched teeth.

"Well, yes."

"So." Chase leaned forward. "You're saying that you'd turn away an innocent child, deny him the best education, simply because his parents weren't married to each other?"

Thergoode flushed with embarrassment. "Well, no, not exactly."

"What then, *exactly?*" There was a deadly calm to Chase's voice that Thergoode couldn't catch.

"Trojan Academy has a high standard, which is—"

"Which is practicing discrimination," Chase cut in as he stood, snatching back the paper. He loomed over the desk, braced his fist on the surface and smiled thinly at the man. "And you seem to forget that your standards include, by law, everyone."

"This is a private school, Mr. Madison."

"And I sit on the board of education, Mr. Thergoode. My company built this school."

Thergoode lost a little more color. "Mr. Madison, if

you'll just relax, we can come to an understanding.'' Thergoode's skin brightened a fraction. "It is a senator's grandchild, after all. And the child isn't born. This could be for nothing, should he—''

Suddenly Chase's eyes darkened, narrowing to mere slits. "Don't even say it.'' The man was digging himself deeper by the second, and Chase wanted to hand him a shovel.

"No, of course not. How thoughtless of me.'' He shuffled papers, and Chase, no calmer than moments before, clamped his hand over fidgeting fingers.

"Process it. And we'll see who is residing at this academy in a couple years.'' He ended the statement with an arched brow, the look menacing. Mr. Thergoode swallowed hard. His Adam's apple bobbing like a slice of broken glass. Chase hoped he cut his throat on it.

Chase left, his anger simmering as he drove back to the construction site. The solid realization that his child would be named a bastard, illegitimate, left a sour taste in his mouth and a foul curse on his lips. Thergoode was just the beginning of what he and Tessa would encounter, of what his child would face. But Chase would do anything to protect his son or daughter, even before they had to face the ridicule of the world. He smacked his fist against the steering wheel in frustration. Telling Tessa wasn't going to be easy. This would hurt her. But in the same instance it might make her see that what she was doing, having a child in this tiny town without a father's name, was going to snowball right to her independent doorstep.

"You didn't.''

Chase nodded.

Tessa stood at the rear of her shop and closed her eyes, waiting for patience to attack her in spades. "I wouldn't want my child in that snob cesspool academy anyway, Chase, and why didn't you at least consult me before doing something so...outrageous? Not that you had the right. I would have said stay out of it.''

She was breathless and rambling, and he liked it. "Make you nervous, don't I?"

"Hah." She snapped through sizes. "What you *do*, Chase Madison, is make me mad enough to spit. How could you give private *details* about me to anyone?" she hissed, not looking him in the eye as she straightened clothes on the racks.

"Hey, it's not like *one* of them isn't obvious." His gaze dropped meaningfully to her belly.

She made a face.

"Having a baby alone was your choice," he whispered, an edge to his tone.

"Yes, it was and I was doing fine, just fine, till you came along."

He wasn't buying that line anymore. "I want my son to have my name. We could change all this gossip in one hour, you know."

"No!" Every customer in the shop glanced at her and she repeated herself, more softly. "No. I don't *need* your name. Lightfoot has done quite well for me and will for my baby." He was only asking for the baby's sake anyway, so her refusal shouldn't make him look as if she'd slapped him. "I can handle anything that comes along. And *you* opened that can of worms, anyway."

She was right, dammit. He wouldn't be here, stewing like a madman, if he hadn't gone to the academy. Yet Chase saw hurt in her eyes, hurt that anyone would think less of their baby because his parents lacked vows between them. But it wasn't going to make her change her mind about marrying him.

"I was wrong, Tessa," he admitted softly, and she met his gaze, his own moving over her dress, the dark teal drape edged in eyelet lace. That's what he thought of when he thought of Tessa, lace and satin and slow, wet sex. His eyes said as much as he shifted even closer, crowding her. She smelled like spice, the fire of her temper lingering in her eyes. "Do you know how beautiful you are?"

"As a cement truck, maybe," Tessa scoffed, yet felt per-

spiration burst on her throat and race down her body. "Of
course, that might be a turn-on, your being in construction,
huh?"

His lips curved seductively. "*You're* a turn-on."

He stood so close to her side, he was practically strad-
dling her hip, his leg brushing over her thigh. His body's
undeniable warmth steamed where they touched, and when
he was close, looking at her as if she were dessert for a
hungry vagrant, she felt her knees soften, her body gravitate
toward him. Tessa licked her lips.

His head dipped, his breath brushing her mouth as he
said, "I'm sorry. I was so eager, I just wasn't thinking."

She gazed into his blue eyes and raised her hand to his
chest. "I know. No real harm done."

The softness of her grazed him, making his groin hard,
and Chase moaned, sinking into her mouth. She reveled in
his wet lips molding over hers and cradled the back of his
head, pressing him harder to her mouth. A tiny sound escaped her and his hand rested at the base of her spine,
rubbing there and lower.

The bell chimed.

Suddenly Tessa jerked back, her face flaming. She sent
him an accusing look, yet Chase grinned despite it. Her
skin was flushed, her lips swollen, the tips of her breasts
pushing against the thin silk fabric of her dress. His gaze
lowered to the evidence, then returned to her face.

"You want me," he said in a low voice.

"No." Immediate, without thought. It was a lie and he
knew it. And it made her angry that her control slipped
whenever he was near. Tessa reminded herself that he was
out for her baby and not her. She couldn't trust him or his
attentions, no matter how handsome and sexy he was, no
matter that her body burned like a fresh fire every time he
touched her. No matter that he kissed like suppressed danger.

"You're doing it again."

"What?" she said as if she didn't know. His wounded

look felt like a kick and she moved away, glancing at her customers and pasting on an innocent smile.

"You're closing me out, suppressing your feelings." His hand closed over her forearm when she wanted to move away, far away from those mysterious eyes. "Because you don't *want* to trust me. Or yourself."

Her gaze flew to his. "You're right, I don't trust you. Or your motives."

Slowly he shook his head. "What you don't trust is what you're feeling."

She scoffed uneasily and to Chase, things got a little clearer.

"You can't push me away, Tessa. I won't go. I'm in your life, and if I have to, someday I'll prove it's *you* I crave. The baby's just an added dividend."

He stared deep into her eyes, holding her prisoner with them, making her feel a lush longing that drove the breath from her lungs. He drank it, in a soft, feathery kiss, a melting of air and scents. He was about to press his mouth harder to hers when she turned her face away and stepped back, clasping her hands in front of her.

Chase felt her distance beyond the three feet separating them.

"It will take more than kisses to make me believe you. And an added dividend? You made it very clear that you want *my* child for *yourself*." Every moment she had to remind herself of that, even when she wanted to stay in his arms. Her voice was frosty and soft when she added, "Don't get any ideas that there's anything more than a little desire between us. My baby and I are one and the same."

His lips tightened in a grim line, his expression angry and determined. "You won't be for long." He spun about and stalked from her shop. Tessa spent the remainder of the day in uneasy confusion, wondering what he'd do next.

A film about King Arthur played on the VCR as Samantha walked into the room, her arms full of small ice cream tubs and spoons.

"Here. Take one of these."

"Give it to Tessa," Dia said. "She has the traveling tabletop." Dia looked pointedly at the plate of takeout pizza perched on Tessa's stomach. She reached for a plate of cookies and Dia snatched them away. "Not good for the baby. Too much caffeine in chocolate, you know."

Tessa slanted her a glance. "At least I have an excuse for big hips," she shot back with a tight smile, taking a double chocolate chip cookie and sinking her teeth into it. Sam laughed and Dia looked down at her body, then instantly put the ice cream aside.

Grinning, Samantha dropped into a stuffed chair, swinging her bare legs over the side, and proceeded to indulge in Jamoca Almond Fudge Decadence.

"Think we should invite Mom?"

The sisters looked at each other, then collectively responded, "Nah."

"The food's not *natural* enough," Dia said, eyeing the pink bucket of ice cream tempting her from the coffee table.

"Natural is good sometimes." Sam's gaze flashed up, her spoon poised at her lips. "This just isn't one of them," she said around a cold mouthful.

"God, she doesn't know what she's missing." Tessa licked the back of the spoon and Dia gave into her weaknesses and ate Rocky Road till she was ill.

"How's it been, living with her these last weeks?" Tessa asked Sam, her smile telling her elder sister she sympathized. Samantha didn't live in New Mexico, but chose to remain in Colorado, where they had all been born and raised. Sam had been her only champion when her mom and Dia tried talking her out of artificial insemination. The distance never stopped Sam from showing up regularly to keep their mother and little sister in line. She had come for an extended visit during Tessa's last trimester, and Tessa adored her for it.

After a moment, Sam shrugged. "Fun, actually. Mom's an incredible woman, very powerful."

Dia and Tessa exchanged a smirking glance, and Tessa

avoided outright laughter by stirring her ice cream. Then she lifted a slice of pizza and took a huge bite. Her mind wasn't on the movie, but on an engineer with an incredible behind.

"How's Chase?" Dia asked casually.

Samantha glanced up.

Tessa blinked, then chewed, washing the food down with diet soda and wondering if they could read her mind as she said, "He tried to get the baby into Trojan Academy."

Sam frowned. "Trojan Academy? Great Goddess, sounds like a condom factory."

Laughter erupted and Tessa agreed.

"More like snob factory," Tessa said. "Costs a fortune in tuition. And this is an elementary school!"

"Did you fight about it?" Dia asked in her courtroom tone.

Did everyone think all they did was argue? "Only that he had no right to do it without asking me."

"It's his kid, too," Dia pointed out the obvious.

Tessa groaned, not wanting to talk about Chase, for the only memory she could recall was the last one from earlier that day, when he had kissed her into stupidity in the middle of her shop.

"He could even set up a college fund if he wanted," Dia continued.

"Shut up, Dia," Sam said. "Do you ever quit being a lawyer? Feelings, emotions, which I'm sure you've forgotten about, drive people to do what they do. Not the lines of the law."

Dia gave her sister a dry "be realistic" look. "In this case, it's best to stick with the law."

"I'm not having this discussion with you now," Sam said in that I'm-the-big-sister tone, glancing at Tessa. Dia stuck her tongue out at her elder sister, the gesture so childish and reminiscent that Sam had to laugh.

"Why don't you just have some wild sex with him?" Sam asked, and Tessa shot her a stunned look.

"Excuse me?"

Sam shrugged. "You're already pregnant, he's not dis-eased—those tests proved that. And you're hot for him."

"I am not."

"Are too," Sam replied easily. "Your face gets beet red every time someone mentions him."

Tessa set the pink ice cream container on her stomach, making circles in the frost on the label with her fingertip. Her voice was low, almost a whisper when she spoke. "Sex with Chase could never be just sex." Her gaze slipped briefly to her sisters. "Not that I am even considering it," she emphasized, then brought her gaze back to the la-bel. Beyond her vision, Dia tapped Sam and nodded. "Sex...well it's a commitment to him, a lifetime." Tessa continued. "He takes everything seriously, except his dumb jokes."

Sam and Dia exchanged another concerned glance.

Suddenly the baby kicked, sending the container of half-melted ice cream tumbling down Tessa's shirt.

She stared at the mess for a second, then shouted, "Field goal!" and threw her arms up like a referee.

Amid the laughter, the door chimed. Tessa waved off her sisters. "I need the exercise," she said, struggling from the couch. "Paper boy probably," she added, wiping at the drips with paper napkins, making it worse as she flung open the door, saying, "Oh, look what I've done!"

"I wish I'd done it," a dark voice said, and Tessa's gaze flew up.

"Chase."

He liked the breathless startle in her voice. "Hi, Tessa."

She recovered quickly. "Out carousing?" Beyond him, she could see a Jeep-load of men.

He shook his head. "My crew. We just finished a house and celebrated with the owners."

Tessa could feel a pressure in her throat, covered her mouth and turned her face away. "Really?" She tried to stop it, but burped anyway.

Chase's brows rose.

"Excuse me," she muttered, flushing red.

And from inside the house came a high-pitched whine of, "Well, wasn't that attractive?"

Smiling, Chase glanced at the window, noticing the curtains ruffling.

"My sisters." She shrugged. "Sam is here. Would you like to meet her?"

"Tessa, no! I look horrible!" her sister shouted.

Chase grinned. "Not now, later maybe." He waved to the curtain and heard a raspy voice say, "Hey, Chase."

"Just as well," Tessa leaned toward the window, her voice elevated. "Because she's out there *on another plane of existence.*"

"Oh ye of questionable faith, Tessa Marie. Why doesn't anyone believe in my powers?" came muffled by the distance. "They work for me!"

"Put a sock in it, Sam." This, Chase recognized, was Dia. The thought of confronting her made him want to leave before she spouted the legalities of visiting Tessa. Dia Lightfoot had a way of looking at a man, chopping him up and deciding where to store the body parts in one glance.

"You're busy." Girl's night, he thought, the scent of pizza wafting from the house. "I'll see you later." He started to turn away.

"Why *did* you stop by, Chase?"

In a heartbeat he was up against her, his arm around her waist, and his mouth on hers. Tessa gripped his shoulders, kissing him back.

"Go for it, Chase," came from Sam.

"Will the plaintiff please get off the defendant's mouth. Now," Dia said, her tone implying ramifications.

Chase broke the kiss for no other reason than he needed air. Lots of it. His chest heaved with the effort to drag some in. "God, I'm addicted to these," he rasped like a revelation and stole another kiss, soft and quick, then spun on his heels and strode down her walk.

Tessa watched him leave, then slipped into her house.

"You shouldn't be seeing him at all, Tessa."

"Cool your jets, will you, Dia?" Sam snapped. "Good

grief, you sure can kill a girl's sex drive in one punch. I
hate to think what you do to a man.''

Tessa looked at Dia, then Sam. ''We need to get this girl
a date.''

Sam slung her arm around Dia, but spoke to Tessa.
''What we need is to get her la—''

''Samantha Lightfoot!'' Tessa cut in, her hands on her
hips. ''I will never get used to the way you just blurt things
out.''

''It's only the truth.'' She shrugged, then looked at Dia,
giving her a quick squeeze. ''So tell your big sister, when
was the last time you cut loose, like in the old days when
I had to drag you from some daring feat or a wild party
with too many boys before Dad found you?''

''Too long,'' Dia muttered sourly, a streak of longing in
her eyes.

Tessa laughed, handing Dia the pint of soft ice cream
and pushing her onto the couch. Sam sank into the chair,
clicking the pause off on the tape in time to see Sir Lancelot
give Queen Guinevere the kiss that rewrote history. Collectively, they sighed dreamily. Then Tessa realized that
one kiss had brought down Camelot.

Three hours later, Tessa left the bathroom, yawning, and
dragging a brush through her hair. She kicked off her slippers, laid the brush aside, then drew the covers down,
switching off the light before slipping into bed. She stared
into the darkness, her fingers moving over her belly. Her
child was sleeping, she thought, then hoped, for she needed
rest. With Chase in her life she expended more energy then
she had keeping him at arm's length. She'd never felt this
confused in her life. He was a caring man, but she didn't
want him near, didn't want him popping by whenever he
wanted as he had tonight. Even if he was a great kisser and
a boost to her ego. Tessa wanted her life back the way it
was.

Like what? Dull, orderly, efficient?

Yes.

Admit it, a voice in her head coaxed. *You like him disturbing your peace.*

No, I don't.

God, what a liar.

She rolled onto her side, stuffed a pillow between her knees and one under her tummy before nearly pounding the stuffing out of a third to get comfortable. She didn't know what to expect from Chase, she thought, sinking her head onto the pillow. And his threat that he wasn't going anywhere and she'd better get used to it tormented her rest. She flinched when the phone rang and glanced at the luminous clock before reaching for the receiver in the dark.

"Yes?"

She knew it was him before he spoke. She sensed him through the line as if he were in the room. Unconsciously, she pulled the covers higher over her body.

"Hi." His voice was a low rasp, whiskey rough, and the single word sang through her like a stroke of his hand.

Tessa swallowed and tried to sound perturbed. "There is a good reason you're calling me at this hour?"

"Yeah, there's something real sexy about talking to a woman when you know she's in bed."

She rolled to her back, staring at the canopy drapes. "You're pitiful, Chase."

"I know." There wasn't a shred of regret in his voice and she could almost see him smile. "Did you have fun tonight?"

"Did you?"

"There you go again, talking around your feelings."

"Yes, I had fun. I ate too much ice cream and *stayed up too late.*"

"Is that a hint?"

"You mean you'd get one that wasn't tied around a boulder dropping on your head?"

He chuckled softly, the sound even more devastating than his smile.

"Good night, Tessa." She could hear the rustle of sheets, the phone scraping against his beard, and she wondered if he slept in the nude. Chase would, she decided, and the image did some splendid things to her body.

A small smile curved her lips and very softly she said, "Good night, Chase."

The line disconnected and Tessa replaced the receiver. But it was a long time before she managed to fall asleep, an honest smile and deep blue eyes following her into her dreams.

Six

"**I** understand, Dia. No, it's all right. I'll manage. Bye."
Tessa hung up the pay phone outside the local community
center and sighed, pressing her forehead to the cool metal
frame. She tried staying mad at her sister for canceling on
such short notice, but Dia's clients were usually at their
most desperate when they called her. She considered calling
Samantha, then remembered it was the eve of the summer
solstice or some other ritual night.

Well, you expected things like this, she reminded herself.
A single mother faced a lot of events alone. She just wished
it wasn't her first Lamaze class.

The other parents filed past her and she took a deep
breath and followed, trying to ignore the mothers-to-be
comparing complaints, the husbands or lovers with arm-
loads of pillows. She failed. Tessa felt like the odd man
out, like when she was ten years old living in a dinky Colorado town, and she was the only girl in her class not invited to Kelly Pembrook's slumber party.

God, are *you* emotional tonight, she thought and blamed out-of-whack hormones.

She strode over to Debbie, the instructor, an energetic woman in her late twenties, who on her first visit to Tessa's shop had convinced her to attend the seminars.

"Tessa!" The two women hugged. "You won't regret this, I swear."

"Good lord, Deb, only you would have the nerve to wear a shirt like that."

Her bright green sweatshirt was emblazoned with a picture of a very pregnant woman desperately trying to cross her legs and the words Breathe! Pant! It's too late for drugs!

"I know, wonderfully tacky, isn't it?"

Tessa agreed; the look was softened by the words Lamaze instructor printed across the back.

"Listen, Deb, my coach bailed on me. Can I still do this first session without one?"

Debbie frowned, then looked across the open room and pointed. "Then who's he?"

Tessa didn't have to look. She felt him instantly, as if his eyes had the power of touch. Part of her, a big part of her, said walk straight out the door. But another part of her wanted, needed to know what the talkative man had said to these people. She refused to admit she was actually glad to see him. Or that she needed him.

"He's been waiting for you. God, he's cute."

She studied Chase as he walked across the massive room, his sneakers squeaking as he stopped to say something to another couple already settled on a mat. Briefly, she wondered if he owned anything but worn, body-molding blue jeans and tight T-shirts. God, she could see the ridges in his stomach.

"Think so?" she asked, sounding a little breathless, even to her own ears.

"Hell, yeah. Your kid's going to be beautiful."

Tessa swung around to look at her friend. "What?"

"Sure, can't you see it?" Deb said, unaware of the anger filling Tessa. "With those genes, and *those jeans*," she emphasized with pure feminine appreciation, "you can't miss."

Someone called to Debbie just then and she moved away as Chase neared, a backpack slung over one shoulder and pillows stuffed under one arm. Tessa wanted to stuff one in his mouth.

"You told them you were the father!" she snapped.

"Hello, Tessa, and how are you?" he muttered dryly, then added, "Sure. Why not? I am."

"Dammit, Chase." She looked at the floor, rubbing two fingers over the space between her eyes. "Do you realize what you're doing to me when you spread it around?"

His eyes narrowed, his hand on his hip. "Why don't you just tell me, so I get it straight." She didn't notice the edge to his voice.

"Well, for starters, I don't know you well enough to pull that story off. Hell, I don't know you at all or I'd have anticipated your showing up here." His gaze darkened dangerously and Tessa harnessed her temper. "I'm not thinking of my reputation. God knows by now it's questionable, but think of the baby, Chase." She gazed imploringly into his blue eyes. "This child has to live here, go to school here. How's it going to be for her if everyone in the neighborhood knows, God forbid," her voice lowered, "that she was artificially conceived."

His features were tight. "*That* was your choice," he reminded her. "And give me *some* credit, Tessa." He was mad, boiling mad, she realized. "Christ, my brothers don't even know about the damn turkey baster."

She blinked. "But...I thought—when they were at the house—?"

"They don't keep in contact enough with me to know my love life, or lack of it," he said, his anger ebbing. "Yes, they know this baby is mine, but not how he was made."

"She."

"Huh?"

"How *she* was made."

Her belligerence made him smile. "Make a difference?"

"Only because you want a boy."

Chase leaned close enough to whisper, "I wouldn't care, Tessa, as long as both of you are all right." She met his gaze. "I swear."

She wanted to believe him, he realized, but the uncertain look he saw far too often in her eyes and a cast of doubt she couldn't hide, warned Chase that Tessa wasn't even close to seeing him as anything but a number on a test tube. Regardless of how they aroused each other to near combustion.

"And I wouldn't do anything to hurt either of you."

But you are, she wanted to say. You're hurting me because I feel like just a processing unit to you. Do you want to be more? a voice asked. And what are you making him feel when you keep reminding him he's just a donor? She nudged the thought away, unable to deal with it now. She was trying her best to stay angry. But with Chase, it was difficult.

"I don't want to make you feel uncomfortable, Tessa," he said after a moment. "I'll go, if you want."

Tessa didn't answer, her gaze scanning the crowded room. Moms carefully lowering to the floor, husbands offering a reassuring kiss or two. For one instant, she regretted coming here. But this was the last Lamaze class in the area for several weeks, the only one that fit her schedule, and she wanted to do this.

Then she realized Chase was leaving. "No!" She caught up and grasped his arm.

He looked down at her, arching a dark brow.

He was going to make her ask, the rat. "Please. Stay." She stole a glance around them. They'd drawn attention and he noticed, smiled into her eyes, then brushed her hair from her forehead as if she were the most precious creature in his life and everything was normal. Hah. Far from it.

"You don't have to stay, but—"

"Thanks, angel," he cut in and meant it.

"How am I supposed to explain you to people?" she asked quietly.

"Not that you have to, but any way you want."

She cast him a sidelong glance. "You mean that?"

"Sure." He wanted Tessa to come out and say he was her baby's father, be proud of it. Hell, he was beginning to think he wanted more from Tessa than she could possibly imagine. But if he told her what he was really feeling, she'd run.

"Come on." He grasped her hand, tugging. "I've got a primo spot all picked out."

"Primo?" Her lips twitched. "Really."

He maneuvered her between the couples toward the rear and dumped the pillows on a section of mat. After unrolling a small blanket, he twisted toward her, offering his hand. Tessa stared at it for a moment, and knew this took their odd relationship to another level. What level she wasn't sure as she tucked her fingers in his, feeling the comforting warmth, the calluses of a man who worked hard for his livelihood. She lowered to the mat, using his shoulder for support, then sighed in a heap.

"God, I feel like such a cow."

His lips twisted in a soft smile. "You look beautiful to me, angel."

She rolled her eyes. "Quit with the flattery, Chase," she said in a low voice. She wouldn't believe it, couldn't. Allowing herself to imagine anything beyond his wanting her baby was ludicrous. But when she couldn't take off her shoes without a strain and he leapt to do it, Tessa experienced a strange burst of emotion. It was a simple yet intimate task, but he did it without a second thought and it forced her to take another, deeper look at this man whose genes she'd selected.

When he found her staring at him, he smiled knowingly and she felt her face warm. He really was *too* cute.

"Here, sit in front of me, then the pillows." He positioned the pillows between them. "Good. Now relax back."

"I don't think that's necessary." She didn't want to be

that near, to smell him, feel him wrapped around her and doubt his every motion. She wasn't ready for that.

"We have to do it this way, Tessa."

She looked skeptical. "I suppose you know a lot about Lamaze?"

"Read a book on it last night."

She blinked. "Why does that *not* surprise me," she said and resolutely let him draw her back between his bent legs. She was grateful for the several inches of down and feathers separating them, but it really didn't help. Chase radiated his own kind of heat.

And she was just getting a good dose of it when a neighboring couple spoke to him and she twisted to listen in. It was a simple parenting-type question—removable car seats or cars with them built in—and it amazed her that Chase knew which he preferred and why. The engineer in him saw only design and logic and safety. Yet as he spoke, she felt herself becoming removed from the conversation, captivated by watching his profile, the genuine interest in his expression. He was so quick with a smile and a joke, she thought, tension slipping from her. And as she joined in the conversation, Tessa only half noticed his hand smoothing over her arm, slow and natural.

"What did you tell them?" she asked a few moments later.

He bent and whispered in her ear, sending a gallop of gooseflesh down her throat to her breasts. "Only that I want to be with you every step of the way during this. What else is there?"

Yeah, what else? Yet she liked that he wasn't offering any information. "You know, when I first started to show, it forced me to answer a lot of uncomfortable questions."

"But you handled it," he said with all confidence.

"Well, I avoided being accurate." Her gaze wavered and her hand rode over her stomach. "I've found people instantly looked at my tummy, my hand for a wedding band, and when they don't see the gold, they immediately feel

it's open season to be nosy." She met his gaze, looking
wounded. "Total strangers asking very personal stuff."

He hated that anyone made her feel uncomfortable about
having their baby and he wanted desperately to protect her
with at least his name. In this day and age he couldn't
believe the gall of some people. But even in the light of
that, Chase knew she wouldn't accept his proposal and he
didn't want to scare her off. Not when she was getting
comfortable with his presence.

"You ought to ask some personal stuff right back, angel.
See how fast they lay off."

Angel. Why was he calling her that? For the eavesdroppers' benefit or for her? Before she could wonder about it,
he nodded toward the front of the room as Debbie introduced herself. He never stopping touching Tessa. If it
wasn't his hand resting on her shoulder with a gentle
weight, it was his thighs cradling her. Almost absently his
fingers stroked her neck or toyed with her braid as they
listened, and Tessa wondered how conscious he was of it,
since he was engrossed in the seminar. But one thing Tessa
realized was how much she missed the touch of a man.
And how much she enjoyed this man's touch.

She got comfortable with him as Debbie showed dia-
grams, offered other birthing techniques, detailed the pro-
cedures after entering the hospital and, most importantly,
described the pain medication options, something Chase
thought she ought to consider.

"No," Tessa said, then flashed him a quick grin. "Of
course, that doesn't mean I won't be shamelessly screaming
for it at the last minute, either."

He did everything that was asked, took notes, and kept
flashing her a funny glad-it's-not-me look when Debbie described birth in more graphic detail. Next time they'd see
a film. Tessa was not looking forward to it. Chase, on the
other hand, couldn't wait.

He asked her opinion on everything and twice they were
hushed for talking too loudly. And Tessa relaxed, *really*

relaxed, for the first time since that day in the lawyer's office three weeks ago.

"I was going to tell them the father died," she confessed during a break.

Chase looked up from the stopwatch he was setting. His expression was blank, unreadable.

She shrugged, a little ashamed. "I couldn't think of a better solution, and you, of course, were not supposed to be involved, especially not like this." She waved at the room of plump moms and eager, nervous dads.

Chase stared at his hand, watching the numbers click off in seconds. She was afraid of him. And he didn't like it. "I'm here now, Tessa, and I want to share this with you, you know that." She nodded minutely. "The last thing I want is to scare you or hurt you." He caught her hand in his, making slow circles over the back with his thumb, watching his movements. "I'm not going to steal this child and run for the hills, angel. I swear on my life, I won't."

He met her gaze and saw the soft sheen of tears in her eyes.

His composure crumbled. "Ahh, Tessa, don't."

She wouldn't let him get closer or hold her like he made to do. "I was just scared, Chase. That's all."

Just scared? More like terrified out of her mind. Yet he let the matter drop and as Debbie instructed, he helped her back into position, stuffing pillows for proper support, then tucked himself behind her. They practiced slow, even breathing, something she was good at, he realized, but when it came to pant-blows, which Chase thought were far too much like a puppy in the middle of summer, she had trouble.

Tessa panted, then blew out a long breath. Sitting beside her, he watched his timer, but watching her was more interesting and he got caught up in matching and coaching her breathing. Tessa panted. Chase panted. And as the imagined contraction increased, she sped up.

Unfortunately, so did Chase.

Then she noticed his skin was flushed, his eyes glassy.

"Chase? Chase, stop," Tessa said, sitting up and reaching for him.

"Whoa!" Then he fell back on his rear and clutched his head.

Tessa laughed softly and offered him water. "Getting into it, huh?"

"More like taking off. God, my head." It was spinning.

Tessa laughed harder and Chase lowered his hands slowly, looking up at her and loving the soft, husky sound. He couldn't get enough of it.

They moved on to the next stage of controlled breathing and when Tessa needed something to focus on, Chase pulled a little frame from his backpack and positioned it near her feet. She inhaled sharply and her gaze flew to his.

It was the sonogram.

Her eyes teared and Chase smiled, yet when she wanted to speak he hushed her, ordering her to concentrate. How could she? He kept pointing to the spot on the printout that *she knew* were fingers and kept saying, "See, a boy," right in the middle of her breathing.

When it was time to relax on her side, he hovered close, adjusting pillows, yet it was the caressing way he positioned her legs, her arms, that made her heart pound. His hands lingered, grew more intimate in their stroking as he massaged her back. Then he tucked himself behind her, torso propped on one elbow, his breathing low and even with hers. Tessa found it hard to focus on anything, except the great-smelling man and the warmth of his body behind her. It was as if they were sharing a bed.

"Tessa?" Chase whispered.

"Hum?" She was so comfortable she didn't want to move.

"Have dinner with me tomorrow night?"

She stiffened, yet his warm hand kept smoothing the length of her arm, nudging it away. "Admit there's something really good between us." She leaned back to look at him, arching a brow. "Besides the baby," he whispered, then ducked even closer. "You knew it the instant we kissed. And kissed.'' He inhaled the wonderful scent of her. ''Hell, Tessa, we came unglued.'' When she simply stared, searching his eyes, he added a safety net. ''It's only dinner. No meeting family, no pressure, just talking.''

His sincerity touched her in a place she'd sworn he'd never reach, and Tessa warred with the reasons keeping her back. Keeping her from enjoying his company like a normal man and woman and not prospective parents. Each reason was vividly clear when she'd walked in here, but now...

She nodded and he smiled, not one of his big, wide, sappy grins, but a slight tugging of his lips. His gaze raced over her face, absorbing every detail, and Tessa felt a difference in this look. Unspeakably intimate. Possessive. Chase Madison was suddenly more dangerous than ever before.

At the end of the session, he rolled the blanket, stacked the pillows, then helped her with her shoes. As he pulled her to her feet, he settled her against him. Their baby moved and Chase felt something clutch in the vicinity of his heart. The large conference room was rapidly emptying, and without warning, he pushed her arms around his neck and kissed her. She didn't pull away, didn't jolt. Instead she accepted, received, almost as if she'd expected it. Chase stole the advantage, lushly tasting her over and over, a gentle, loving kiss that made her toes slowly curl.

She drew back, breathless, warm. ''Chase.'' She glanced to see if anyone was watching.

He didn't care. ''I like kissing you.''

Her guard went up and she stepped out of his arms. ''You said just dinner.''

''Yeah, tomorrow, but today isn't over yet.'' He gathered their things.

''Great job, Chase,'' Debbie called as they left the center.

''Teacher's pet,'' Tessa teased. ''I actually think you enjoyed this.'' She wanted his mind off that kiss and onto anything else.

But he was wise to it. ''You didn't?''

She shrugged, then sent him a glance behind loose tendrils of dark hair. "Of course, watching you nearly hyperventilate yourself into a coma was certainly interesting."

His face darkened a bit. "Pinching you had its merits." He stopped beside her Jeep, not ready to end this night with her.

"I didn't notice." It was supposed to be a focal point of pain, but he never did more than squeeze her arm.

"I hardly think anything will be an equal pain setting when the time comes."

She looked down at her stomach, laughing nervously. "I want this so bad, always have, but when I look at this huge belly I think, 'This baby has to come out and there's only one way,' and I get a little scared."

Inwardly he winced, but kept it well-hidden. "You can do it. You're tough, Tessa." Women, he decided, possessed a much higher pain threshold than men to suffer through what Debbie had just described. And without screaming for drugs. Lots of them. Good ones.

She scoffed. "Yeah, right. You should have seen me when I was being inseminated."

That brought him up short. He couldn't imagine the process, but he wanted to know. But what he wanted more than anything was to show sexy Tessa Lightfoot how God intended them to procreate. You're a hopeless mess around her, he thought ruefully. "You'll have to tell me about that tomorrow." He helped her into the Jeep, waiting until she locked herself in. "I'm going to follow you," he hollered beyond the sealed glass.

The window lowered on a buzz. "Chase. I'm perfectly capable."

He nodded and reminded himself that they'd made progress tonight and not to push it. "See ya."

"Thanks, Chase."

"There's nothing I wouldn't do, angel."

He was right, she thought.

There wasn't anything he wouldn't do. For his child.

* * *

Chase stood at the entrance to the stockroom of Tessa's Attic, peering over the edge of wooden crates to watch the proprietress attempt to draw something from the bottom of a deep box. Her tummy was in the way. Yet he didn't move to help, not yet. He was busy admiring her long, muscled legs and the sweet bottom wrapped in a pale pink leather miniskirt. Only Tessa could pull that off while pregnant, he decided, grinning when she used a broom handle to drag whatever she wanted up. When that failed, she tried tipping the box. When she resorted to twisting a coat hanger into a hook, he spoke up.

"Can I help?"

She popped upright, shoving hair from her face, her eyes wide as coins. "What are you doing here?"

He moved around a stack of boxes. "Enjoying the scenery."

She flushed red. "Right." Dry, amused, she adjusted her skirt. Then she frowned, glancing at the clock. "I thought you said dinner."

He shrugged like a bashful boy. "I have to cancel." He actually liked the disappointment in her eyes. "But I've come to renegotiate," he said, moving to her side and peering in the box. He smiled at her, wiggling his brows. "Nice," he said, then bent and lifted out the sexiest scrap of lingerie he'd ever seen. It was a white eyelet lace bra and panties, delicate, innocently transparent. He looked her over, thoroughly, suggestively, and she knew he was trying to picture her in the set.

"Forget it, Madison," she said, snatching it back. "I could barely get a thigh in this thing." She tossed it on a stack of others in various colors. "You mentioned negotiations?"

"I have a business dinner, very dull." His expression was suddenly hopeful. "Unless, of course, you'd like to come along?"

"With your business associates? I don't think so."

"Yeah, I figured that much."

She folded her arms over her tummy. "What's the deal?"

Glad she hadn't totally dismissed the idea of spending time with him, he reached out and brushed her hair off her shoulder, his gaze lingering over the lacy white blouse and long pink vest. The hint of more lace taunted him from the shadows of the blouse. He wanted to peel away every expensive layer, slowly.

"Come with me now."

She arched a brow, his feathery touch driving through her like streaks of heat.

"What do you say?"

"I can't. I have work to do." She waved at the cluttered storeroom.

"So do I, but it's lunchtime and Dana said you haven't taken a break all morning."

"Dana needs to keep her mouth shut."

"Just go for it, Tessa." He moved closer, dangerously close, and slid his arms around her waist. "Drop everything and come with me. Now."

She pried his hands free and stepped away. He was getting too comfortable. All last night she'd relived his kisses, the warmth and strength in his touch. And Tessa knew, the more he touched her, the weaker she'd get. He only wants the baby, she reminded herself.

"You're assuming a lot, Chase," she said in a guarded voice.

"I assume nothing but this." He reached and caught her against him, instantly covering her mouth with his. Her resistance lasted seconds and her answer nearly undid him. Her arms wrapped around his neck, her mouth grinding against his, her fingers plowing into his hair. Her body arched to him and when she couldn't get close enough, she moaned with frustration. Then he shifted and she did feel him, the masculine hardness pressing to her hip, telling her the truth, telling her that she excited him as much as he did her.

His back braced against a high table, his broad hands

smoothed over her back as his mouth moved over hers, thick and heavy with desire. He shaped her hips, the curve of her buttocks, his fingers grazing the skin of her thighs. He felt the lacy tops of her stockings, the kind without garters, and the image drove through his brain like a shaft of steel. God, he wanted her. Now. Right now.

"Tessa, ah, angel," he said against the flesh of her throat, leaving a trail of kisses. "Don't you see? Can't you feel this?"

Tessa tried to talk, but all that came out was a strangled "Yes." Reality was hard to face. He was right. And she loved, how she *loved* that he desired her, even in her present condition. Then he kissed her again, lush and deep, and her hands explored the width of his chest, the flatness of his stomach hidden beneath the green banded-collar shirt. His muscles jumped to her touch and, against his lips, she smiled.

"I want you," he breathed into her mouth. He insinuated his knee between her thighs, settling his hands on her buttocks and drawing her along the length of his leg, and she gasped, dropping her head back and clutching his shoulders.

The warmth of her sex seared him.

She wanted to be closer. He bent and rubbed his mouth against the hollow of her throat, his lips nudging the fabric aside. When he touched the sensitive swells of her breasts, Tessa thought she'd liquefy onto the floor.

"Chase. Oh, Chase." She was extrasensitive to his touch, to her reactions, and knew him for a special sort of man when his hand caressed over her belly as if it were flat and smooth. Then it drove lower, his rough palm sliding down her thigh, then back up, beneath the skirt.

And Tessa let him, her body clamoring with a thousand tingling sensations, her mind conjuring erotic images of him pushing her skirt up and making love to her right there.

Then he did, hooking his knee inside hers and spreading her. His palm covered her womanhood, a possessive claim, and Tessa's body exploded with moisture. He dragged his fingertip up the length of her panties to the edge, feeling the heat and dampness.

"Tessa." He drew her name out, a slow hiss of wonder. "You're so hot."

"I know," she moaned half in wonder, her mouth thick and draining on his. "Oh, God. We shouldn't be doing this." But it was wonderful, feeling the rush of desire unequaled by anything she'd experienced before. She wanted desperately to explore it.

For an instant, Chase could hear everything, her breath, the shift of her stockinged leg against his jeans, the rustle of fabric beneath her vest and blouse. As if the world ceased beyond this moment, no sound penetrated, time and energy focusing down to them, pressed so tightly together.

"I want to touch you, angel," he rasped darkly. "I swear I'll go mad if I don't."

"Chase." She swallowed, licked her lips and kissed him again, pulling at his shoulders, a silent signal of urging.

Delicately he pushed the fabric aside. He found her, wet and smooth as velvet. As his fingers sank into her, she shrieked against his mouth, jolted by the erotic contact, his probing touch. But Chase felt her climbing the wall of her passion, a rapid journey neither could stop, and he wished he were inside her now, his body stroking hers. His thumb circled the throbbing bead of her. She clawed at his shoulders, straining against his hand.

A whimper caught on his tongue as it swept inside her mouth.

She drenched him with her desire, pulsed with it.

Her nails dug deeply, then her arms slid around his neck, tight and imprisoning. Her hips rocked. And Chase kept kissing her, swallowing her deep, fluid groans, absorbing her shudders as she was suddenly wild in his arms.

He almost lost himself just feeling it.

For several moments, she was tense against him, her breathing soft and rapid, then, like the ebb of a wave, she sagged against him, burying her face in the curve of his throat.

An instant later, the door burst open.

"Oops." Dana flushed and smiled, backing out and closing the door.

Chase held her tightly when she wanted to leave his arms, removing his hand and smoothing her skirt, settling her more firmly to her feet.

"Oh God. I'm so embarrassed," she mumbled against his skin. "For Dana to see me—us—"

"Shhh," he hushed, pushing her hair back. "She didn't see anything, angel, except you in my arms. There are too many boxes shielding us."

The scent of her mingled with her perfume and Chase thought he could live in the fragrance. His mouth met hers again, softer this time.

And Tessa didn't think she could look this man in the eye without thinking of the pleasure he gave her, unselfishly, erotically. He has to be hurting right now, she thought, feeling his arousal thick in his jeans.

"Come with me, Tessa," he said into her mouth. "Trust me." He stepped back and away, moving to the door, though it was a strain, the ache in his groin painfully obvious. He was going to finish this if he didn't get them a change of scenery. He paused at the door, his hand on the knob as he faced her. He held out his hand. "Trust me."

Tessa swallowed repeatedly, trying to catch her breath and look him in the eye. For a moment she felt shame over what they'd done, but as she lifted her gaze to his, his tender expression, the desire and compassion in his eyes sent her misgivings away like a leaf on a breeze. She didn't want to think anything so good could be a mistake, that he'd given her such unbelievable pleasure with anything but her in mind.

Chase's heart did a quick flip when she walked toward him, her hand out to accept. He pulled her against him and kissed her again, deep and utterly possessive.

"You won't regret this, angel."

I hope not, she thought, then slipped into the bathroom to repair her appearance. She stared at her reflection in the mirror. Her lips were red and swollen, her skin pink from his whiskers, and her eyes were unusually bright.

"You're a tart. A pregnant tart," she told her image, yet she couldn't remember the last time she'd felt like this. As she brushed out her hair, securing it off her neck in a bow, excitement rushed through her again. He was on the other side of the door, waiting. Was he afraid she wasn't coming out?

She started when she found Chase leaning against the door frame, his smile knowing, and she felt her cheeks warm as his gaze caressed her.

"I liked the ravished look better," he murmured, then he grabbed her hand.

They moved briskly through the shop, customers and employees staring, Tessa tossing Dana orders to hold down the fort as Chase dragged her out to the street. Sunlight sprayed them with warmth, and she smiled.

Tessa was not usually a reckless person. Her sisters and mother insisted she was an alien offspring because she planned her days and life with meticulous order. But Tessa took one look at Chase's handsome face and knew that being reckless with him, this once, just might change her for life.

Seven

From the passenger seat of his Grand Cherokee, Tessa watched Chase slide carefully behind the wheel. His discomfort was obvious and something hot and sexy slithered through her with the knowledge that she had created it, aroused him till it showed. And showed.

He buckled up and turned the key, except he didn't pull into traffic and instead, gripped the steering wheel, taking deep breaths.

"Chase? You okay?"

"No." He glanced sideways, his eyes half lidded, glistening dark. "You're dangerous when you ignite, Tessa."

Her expression softened, color flooding her cheeks. No one had ever said that to her, and definitely not with such a seductive threat.

Then he leaned over and cupped the back of her head and drew her to his mouth. "I like it," he said against her mouth, then kissed her, warm and wet.

Me too, she thought with a jolt of reality.

He signaled, pulling the car into traffic. "I need a cold shower. A long one."

Tessa propped her arm on the back of the seat and let her gaze slip over him. "So I noticed."

He glanced at her, then made a right turn. "And if you keep looking at me like that, I'll show you more."

Her brows shot up onto her forehead.

"I do want you, Tessa. All of you."

"Chase," she said uncomfortably.

"Too soon?"

She nodded, feeling guilty and selfish.

Chase shifted in the seat, the crowd in his jeans uncomfortable. He warned himself that Tessa might have exploded in his arms, but that was a long way from letting him in her bed. "I'm notorious for my patience. And of course, lately, cold showers."

She laughed at that and he gave her a sour look, amused and frustrated. As he slid the car into a parking slot and shut off the engine, she was surprised to see they were at the park. He hopped out of the car and came to her side, making her close her eyes. With the excitement in his expression, she couldn't deny him the game. Whatever he was up to, he was just too pleased with himself. When she opened them, Chase had a picnic laid out on a thick quilt, with four pillows, two propped against the tree.

"You knew I'd say yes?"

"I hoped. If you didn't, I want you to know I was prepared to resort to gratuitous begging." He flashed her that grin as he emptied the basket, then popped open a can of juice for her, a soda for himself. Within minutes she was comfortably ensconced against the tree, sharing food with a handsome engineer.

"Why did you choose to be artificially inseminated?"

Tessa lowered the sandwich from her mouth and with it went her gaze. She debated over the wisdom of telling him, then decided she had nothing to lose with the truth. She gave him the details of her life with Ryan, her miscarriage and the subsequent end of her marriage years before.

Anger lit his expression, anger on her behalf, as she said, "He never cared for an instant that his child was gone. Only wanted me and our life back just the way it was. He was too selfish to see we could never go backward after that."

"He was an idiot, Tessa."

"I like to think so," she said with a wry smile.

"You're going to be a great mother."

She smoothed one hand over her belly and took a bite of her sandwich. Mother. She'd waited and wanted so long and the words spilled from her lips. "I hated Ryan and for a long time I blamed him for the miscarriage. When I finally got over him, I decided that I didn't need him nor any man in my life to have what I wanted. And after a few years, I proved it." She watched her hand slide over the sphere of unborn life tucked beneath her vest and blouse, and Chase was mesmerized by the movements of his child shifting inside. "The clinic was the best option, other than risking disease and deceiving a man with casual sex."

"Why me? Or rather my donation," he added with a sour look. The more he thought of test tubes and cold examining rooms, the more he disliked it.

She glanced up briefly, holding his warm, blue gaze. "Well, beyond coloring that was exactly opposite of Ryan, it was nothing more than a feeling."

His features tightened with surprise.

"Must be my mother's influence. But I'd never tell her that." She shrugged. "Mother is rather…spiritual."

Chase's smile widened. "New Age?"

She laughed shortly. "More like another universe." She finished off her sandwich and dusted her fingertips, then her tummy. "No, no more," she groaned when he offered her a paper plate full of fruit. She sank down on her elbow, propping her head in her palm. She watched him eat, or rather devour the last of the sandwiches and fruit.

Beyond them was a baseball diamond and playground equipment shaped like a castle, with tire swings, chain bridges and children everywhere, swinging, running, screaming with laugher. Chase watched it for a moment, then turned to her. She could see it in his eyes, that need to share their energy. And when a baseball landed close and rolled, he reached for it as a boy of about eight came hunting after it.

"Hey, coach. Whatcha doin' here?" The boy's gaze shot to Tessa, her tummy, then to Chase.

"Hi, Jason, got a game going?" Chase offered him a bottle of water.

The boy wiped his sweaty face on his sleeve, then drank. "Yeah, me and the guys thought we'd practice." Chase and Tessa exchanged a smile. "Wanna play? We could use a pitcher. Tommy ain't—isn't—" he corrected when Chase eyed him "—very good today. He wiped out on his bike at school."

Chase tossed the ball up and down, then shook his head. "No, thanks. Go for a long one." Chase drew his arm back.

Tessa stopped him. "Go play."

He shook his head.

"I can see it in your face, *Coach* Madison. You want to. I'm okay just watching."

He looked at Jason waiting for the throw, then to the boys coming off the diamond to see what delayed their all-important practice. "You sure you don't mind?"

She took the ball, rose up on her knees and threw. It went high and long, and Jason had to back-step to catch it.

Chase was stunned and his wide eyes said as much. "Nice arm, Lightfoot."

"Shortstop, two years running, city league," she said with a touch of smugness.

He leaned close and kissed her. "Just a few minutes," he whispered, then called, "Hey, guys, wait up."

Tessa sank onto the pillows and quilt as Chase walked onto the grassy field, rolling up his sleeves. It was clear they all knew him, and soon they were deep into hitting some great shots. He remained bent over, hands braced on his knees, clapping occasionally, and his deep voice carried to her. When one child smacked the ball out of the field,

Chase whooped like a fan, tousling the boy's hair, his expression fatherly proud. The sight of him, so comfortable and happy, made her heart trip. He praised the boys for every good hit, for their form, and when he stepped in to offer advice, adjust a grip, he encouraged. He was too good to be true, she thought, full and suddenly tired.

An hour later, Chase stood over her, drinking water, absently waving to his team as they mounted bicycles and rode home for dinner. She looked contented as she slept, her black hair loose from the bow and spread across the pillow. Her position on her side made her skirt ride up, and he valiantly tossed a blanket over those incredible legs. He sat down beside her, near her feet, and watched her sleep.

The muscles around his heart clenched as their child moved inside her, yet she slept on.

Chase was in trouble. Deep, dangerous trouble. He'd known it the instant he heard her laugh for the first time, saw her eyes gloss with tears. She was strong and independent and it killed her to trust him, even for a moment. But she did. She kissed like magic and erupted like…like an earthquake. He'd never felt this way about a woman before, not even with Janis. The two women were so completely different, he wondered now what he'd ever seen in his ex-wife. Everything about Tessa attracted him—the way she tilted her head when she questioned him, the cute habit she had of biting her lower lip when she was nervous or indecisive. He wanted to know more, like what she looked like when he made love to her, the expression on her face when his body brought hers to the threshold of desire. What it felt like to be moving inside her.

He recalled the moments in the storeroom and, though he would have preferred more privacy, he couldn't forget how her skin felt beneath his mouth, his fingers. The scent of her lingered on him and he loved it. God, if she only knew how close he had been to opening his jeans and pushing into her. Silently, he commended himself on his restraint and wondered how long it would last. Loving Tessa was better than breathing.

She stirred, and he changed the direction of his thoughts before the whole park full of people saw him make a fool of himself. "Tessa?" he called softly.

She woke, yawning and stretching, then jolted upright, lightly slapping her leg. "Ow, ow! Cramp. *Bad* cramp!" she cried, her look imploring him for help.

He came to his knees, cradling her calf in his thighs and digging his thumbs into the tight muscle. The blanket slid away, but Tessa didn't care. All she wanted was the clenching to stop, and then it did.

"Thank you," she breathed, his fingers still manipulating the muscle. "Uh, Chase?" She lifted herself up on her elbows and met his gaze. "It stopped."

"I know."

"Then let go."

He didn't. Instead he sank to the quilt, drawing her legs over his, and kept massaging her calves, ankles and feet. "You don't stretch out enough when you do your walks."

So male, she thought. An answer for everything. "I'm pregnant is the cause. Cramps are common. I'm carrying extra weight, hormones, et cetera, et cetera," she waved, yet it felt good. Her circulation was always the pits when she first woke up. "How was the game?"

"Jason was great. Timmy and Stephen need to work on their fielding, but I think we'll—"

He glanced up. She was smiling.

"Please tell me you have some faults, Chase Madison."

"My mother would kill to hear you say that."

"Well?"

"I've been known to eat over the sink and drink milk straight from the carton."

She waved that one off. "A guy thing. I want the dirt."

He looked at the sky, thoughtful.

"Oh, come on," she said, shoving him with her foot.

He grinned. "I squeeze the toothpaste from the middle," he said hopefully.

"Not good enough. I do too."

"I rarely sort laundry?"

She shook her head.

"I sleep in the nude?"

Her gaze slid lazily over him. *That* she'd like to see. "More."

"What do you want to know, Tessa? That I have a temper and it's taken me years to control it? That I'd rather work with my hands than in an office?" Those hands caressed her legs, distracting her. "That I avoid bars and nightclubs because I used to drink too much, hate living alone, and prefer videos to theaters?" Not satisfied, she urged him on. "Or that I plan my winter schedule around a hunting trip Colin and I take to Christian's place every year like clockwork, whether Christian likes it or not?" He leaned over her. "Or that I have one fault you won't believe."

"And that is?" she said, breathless with his nearness.

"I can't stop thinking about you and I want you in my bed, in my life."

A ripple of excitement roared through her. "A crime, I'm sure," she managed.

His brows rose.

"Why?" she finally said, gesturing to her tummy.

His expression softened and he lay beside her, his torso propped on his bent elbow. "I see beyond this, Tessa. Way beyond." He ran his hand familiarly over her belly and she caught it, stopping him. "And right now I'm so hot for you, if we were alone, you wouldn't get away."

"Is that a fact?" Her gaze shifted to his mouth, then back to his eyes. Feminine satisfaction raced through her.

He grasped her hand and beneath the rumpled blanket he pressed her palm to his arousal. "Fact."

Tessa gasped, a soft ragged burst. Her eyes closed. Her fingers flexed. Chase moaned. The image of him bare for her touch, their bodies entwined, bloomed in her mind. She opened her eyes and stared directly into his. His mouth was inches away.

"We definitely need to take this somewhere more private."

She jerked her hand back and sat up suddenly. Her? In his bed? The thought of him seeing her nude, like *this*, scared her.

"It's late, Chase, and Dana's been left alone too long."

Frowning, he sat up, touching her arm. "Tessa? Look at me." She wouldn't.

She busied herself with folding a blanket. "It's my shop, and neglecting it doesn't pay the bills. I have to restock inventory and there's jewelry to order." She knew she was rambling, but his words were laced with a commitment that was ludicrous to consider now.

But she didn't want to give up this day, not yet. She liked him a lot more than she'd ever anticipated, more than was wise, and she felt a strange pulling in the pit of her stomach when his fingers slid into her hair, tilting her head to look into her eyes.

"I'm a patient man, Tessa." The message was clear. This wasn't over. Not by a long shot. He drew her closer. He was going to kiss her again, give her that seductive energy he radiated. And when he did, she pulled him flush to her body and sank to the blanket with him in her arms. She didn't care that people watched, didn't care that his hands were where they shouldn't be. She wanted him to hold her.

"Chase Madison!"

The voice was strident and commanding. They broke apart and sat up to find Dia Lightfoot, in severe black and tall heels, staring down at them. No, not staring, glaring.

"What are you doing to my sister!"

"Has it been *that* long, Dia, that you can't remember?" Tessa asked before Chase could respond.

Chase's lips twitched to hold back a smile as he helped Tessa to her feet. Tessa motioned to Dia, who was glaring at Chase, and the two sisters spoke privately. Chase would have given his eyeteeth to hear the conversation and decided to make himself scarce with repacking the Jeep.

"Are you crazy?" Tessa's sister demanded.

"Dia. Get a grip."

"This is so unlike you."

"What? Kissing a man."

"No, kissing *that* man, in the park, in broad daylight, where everyone in town can see!"

Tessa planted her hands on her hips. "So." She didn't have to explain herself to anyone, least of all her kid sister. "God, Dia, what's happened to you? You used to be the one to instigate trouble, be reckless."

"That was then and this is now. Well?"

"Well, what?"

"Just what were you doing, besides kissing?"

Tessa blinked. "That's none of your business and tell me that's not the reason you hunted me down."

"No, Dana was worried and called. You've been gone all afternoon."

Tessa glanced at Chase as he finished loading the Jeep. "Yeah, I know."

"Careful, Sis."

Tessa frowned at her. "You were the one who said I should get to know him."

"Sure, so he wouldn't sue for custody. But that—" she waved to the spot near the tree "—is more than I meant."

"Afraid I'll stain your reputation?" Dia was the first of her family to oppose her decision to artificially inseminate.

That stung, and Dia knew the source. "No matter what I've said in the past, Tessa, it's you I worry about. You're vulnerable."

"Pregnancy does *not* make me stupid, Dia," she said, folding her arms over her stomach. "I know what I'm doing."

"It's the *with whom* I'm worried about."

"You need a break, Dia. Badly," she said, and left her sister standing on the grass, her expensive pumps sinking into the soft dirt. Tessa stopped beside Chase.

"I feel like a kid caught in the back seat of his daddy's car," he said.

She slanted him a glance. "You speaking from experience?"

"Nah, Dad never let me use his car. I had to buy my own and that didn't happen till I was in the Marines."

"Not in college?"

"Marines first, college came later." He shook his head, rueful. "I'm the black sheep of the family, you know."

"You?"

He grinned. "A fault you like?"

Her lips twitched. "Only if it doesn't carry over into genes." She rubbed her tummy.

"Yeah well, going into the Marines ticked my dad off good. Not following in the family dynasty didn't help, either."

Chase's father was a politician, she recalled, a retired senator or something. "And now?"

"God, I hope he's over it," he said dryly, amused.

Tessa laughed uneasily, not ready to meet his parents. That was just a little too deep. They climbed into the car.

"Your sister upset you?" He inclined his head toward Dia.

Tessa shook her head. "She's just wound up a little too tight these days." Tessa glanced out the window and Dia waved, offering her sister an I-hope-you-forgive-me smile as she slipped into her red Mercedes.

"She was mad, Tessa."

She sighed, brushing dry bits of grass from her blouse. "She warned me that I'm oh-so-vulnerable while carrying her niece."

"Family has a right to worry."

"Do yours?" Instantly she wished the words back.

Chase scoffed happily. "My mom is champing at the bit to meet you and Dad claims that his first grandson is destined to be president."

Tessa immediately looked out the window, unexpected tears filling her eyes as she realized how her decision, her baby, was affecting so many people. Yet he'd never reminded her of anything but his own concern. She knew this was his family's first grandchild, an occasion they should be involved in, and she was cutting them off. Even her own family was sort of lax about the baby. As if they weren't sure they could love a baby made with a stranger's sperm donation. But Chase, she knew beyond doubt, loved this child.

He pulled into a slot before her shop, and she was discreetly drying her eyes when he opened her door. Immediately, he frowned. "Angel?"

She slid from the seat. "I had a wonderful day, Chase. Thank you."

When she wouldn't look at him, he tipped her chin. "Was it something I said?"

She rested her hand on his broad shoulder. "No. I think I just need some time to think."

He nodded and knew she meant without him around. He ducked and brushed his lips to hers and she clung to him, fighting back tears and kissing him deeply.

"I'm sorry," she whispered, and he thought she meant about crying.

But Tessa realized she was being selfish and cruel and that keeping Chase out of her life, at this moment, wasn't fair, no matter how much it might hurt her later. And as she left him and entered her shop, she realized that she no longer thought of him as a donor, or even her baby's father, but as her man.

During the next week, Tessa saw Chase every day, even if it was just for a few moments between picking up supplies for his jobs. Half the time he was covered with dirt and sweat and he'd steal a wet, smacky kiss, then head out, unmindful of his crew hooting from the back of a truck. Madison Construction built homes, she discovered, one at a time, customized. She admired the fact that he'd started out doing it alone, a one-man operation with no financial help from his father.

One day when he didn't show at her shop, she worried, but still couldn't bring herself to call his office or home.

"I missed you today, angel. I have a game after work. Call you later," was the message on her answering machine.

Tessa listened to it twice, missing him.

Eight

Chase turned his head to spit and nearly choked when he saw Tessa sitting in the bleachers. He grinned and missed his best player hitting a line drive to second base. He couldn't believe she was here. *Here.* And he had difficulty concentrating with his heart beating so hard in his chest. He called his player home, then strode toward the stands. She climbed down and met him at the fence, her fingers in the links. The fence came to just below her chin.

"Do you mind?" she asked hesitantly.

"Hell, no!" He resisted the urge to drag her across the fence and into his arms. "How long have you been here?"

"Since the second inning." That surprised him, since it was the ninth now. "You've got a good team," she said, looking out over the sea of blue jerseys and caps in the Mustang dugout before bringing her gaze back to his. She made a disgusted face. "Tell me that isn't tobacco in your mouth, Chase."

He blew a huge bubble, popped it, then sucked the pink gum back into his mouth.

"Worried about my health?"

Yeah, she was. But she wasn't going to puff up his already pleased look. She reached out to rub gum stuck to his lip.

It was a wifely thing to do, almost motherly, and he wanted this mother. Her navy blue bike shorts and sneakers showed off her shapely legs and the matching shirt, simple and loose, draped her softly. Her hair was twisted in a knot on her crown, the early summer heat dampening strands at her neck and temple. She looked good enough to eat. And he told her so.

"God, I love how you blush," he said on a laugh, then leaned closer. "What do you taste like, I wonder?"

"Sugar and spice?" she said.

"Have I mentioned I like spice? Lots of it," he said with a velvety look.

Her heart pounded with the idea of Chase tasting every inch of her. Slowly.

The umpire called for a batter.

"Go play, little boy," she said, giving him a shove, but Chase brushed a kiss to her knuckles before he turned away, his cleats digging into the dirt. Her gaze unwillingly dropped from his wide shoulders to his tight behind shifting in the dark uniform trousers. Nice, Madison, real nice, she thought and stayed there for a moment, suddenly feeling a hundred pairs of eyes drilling into the back of her head. She didn't want to turn around and see the faces of parents. While she was worried earlier about explaining him to her friends, she hadn't thought of how her very pregnant presence here could affect his position as peewee coach. Their dating, if that's what one could call the progression of their odd relationship, wasn't easily explained. But in the next instant, Tessa didn't care. She hadn't listened to anyone but herself since her divorce and she wasn't going to let a few curious stares get to her. She knew she'd been uptight about their situation and anyone discovering the means of her pregnancy, but things had changed. Their relationship had shifted, somehow felt more secure. She was proud of her child and her feelings for Chase and as she returned to her seat in the stands, she smiled to herself.

Well, for heaven's sake. She didn't know exactly when it had happened, but she'd fallen hard for that man. Or rather tripped, she thought with a dose of reality, her heart tumbling into the hands of a smiling engineer. He'd wormed his way into her life with all the finesse of a Brahman bull, bossy and determined, and she couldn't go a minute without thinking about him, about kissing him or feeling the warmth of his arms around her. For the past several days they'd spent only small amounts of time together, nothing like in the storeroom, yet it was time filled with more than getting to know him, but getting to love him. She leaned forward and braced her elbows on her knees, her eyes on him and not the game.

Oh, God.

Did she?

Something else stuck her just as quickly. Did *he* love her? Was their relationship progressing *because* of their child or *in spite* of it? If the baby wasn't between them, would she feel this good about him? She let the questions torment her for all of ten minutes, then decided there was nothing she could do about it. She wasn't honestly certain she loved him at all, or whether what she was feeling was simply because he was a great guy or her child's natural father. Yet when the whistle blew at the end of the game, Tessa pushed her uncertainties aside and met him at the dugout. He was shoving equipment into a heavy canvas sack.

"I'll catch you later," she said.

He straightened and frowned. "You're leaving?" She liked the almost childlike disappointment in his eyes.

"I thought you'd go celebrate." She waved to the dozen eight-year-old boys ribbing each other over their victory.

"Not till the championship. And that's only if they work hard," he said, loudly enough to get their attention. The boys looked up at him as if he were a god, waiting. "Now, that was giving one hundred percent, guys." A collective grin spread through the group. "I'm proud of you. Now go." He inclined his head and they took off.

Parents passed him, herding their children toward the cars as Chase slung the long sack over his shoulder and accepted congratulations, dumping all the praise back on their kids. When she tried to slip away, he caught her, slinging his arm over her shoulder. He introduced her to the parents as they walked to their cars, ignoring their curious stares, keeping the conversation light. Tessa realized that Chase Madison wasn't offering anyone a piece of his private life.

And she loved him for it.

He stowed his gear, searching the lot for her Jeep.

"I walked."

He blinked. "That's got to be five miles."

"Four and six-tenths. Give me a lift back?" He grinned, and she cupped his jaw, giving it a shake. "You are so readable, Chase Madison."

He covered her hand with his, puckering his lips. "Read this?"

She kissed him, then opened his car door and climbed in. "I'm hungry."

"You're always hungry."

"Don't you think you should feed me?"

His piercing gaze caressed her hotly. "I want to do more than *feed* you, woman," he murmured in a husky voice.

"Chase!"

"Yes," he said innocently.

"That was…ah—?"

"True." He shut the door and within minutes they were heading down the street toward his house. He needed a shower, and though she liked a little sweat on a man, dripping with it was a bit much. She wanted to see his place anyway and was surprised by the modest Cape Cod.

"Before you ask, no, I didn't build it. Janis owned it."

Bitterness weighed his tone, and, once inside, she asked about it.

"I was trying to sell it when I found out about the baby. I decided to hold on to it, rent it maybe."

"That's not what I meant. You have a lot of hate inside you for her."

Chase removed his cleats and crossed the living room, not answering. Finally he dropped the shoes into a wooden box inside the hall closet and shut the door.

"Tessa, I have something to tell you, and, well—"

Her heart jumped to her throat and stayed there. "Just say it, Chase."

"Janis was the administrator of the fertility clinic."

"I know."

He looked at her, his brows high.

"Dia mentioned it. And yes, I thought that she had a hand in the mix-up, but what does it matter now? Blaming her or blaming anyone doesn't change this." She patted her tummy.

"I hate to think she did it to you just to get back at me. She knew how much I wanted to be a dad."

She spoke as she crossed to him. "If she did, it backfired." He met her gaze and she thought he looked a little lost right now. Brushing damp hair off his forehead, she whispered. "You *are* going to be a dad, Chase."

His gaze swept her face and he wrapped his arm around her, pulling her gently against him. "I want to be more than that, Tessa." Before she could respond, he kissed her, so thick and heavy she felt her knees soften and her body spring to life. Then he released her and went down the hall, stripping off his shirt. She fell back against the wall and sighed, and a moment later heard the shower running.

She closed her eyes, her mind conjuring the image of him stripping down to his skin, stepping beneath the spray, lathering that fantastic body, and before she went into his room to see the sight for real, she turned back down the hall.

A little imagination was a dangerous thing, she thought.

She strolled through the house, noting paraphernalia from his time in the Marines, trophies, photos of his family.

Something struck her odd about a woman she thought was his mother, but she couldn't place it.

Stacks of baby books and parenting magazines littered the coffee table. A page was marked in one and she flipped it open, her body doing strange things at the illustration of a man making love to a pregnant woman. Even as she thought of doing that with him, it scared her, made her face burn with embarrassment. She knew he was only thinking of her. It was a shocking thought—how much one man could care—and she wondered about his faults, the temper he claimed was ferocious. She didn't want to see it.

She closed the book and glanced around the living room. The furniture was classic, modular, his collection of audio and video electronic equipment astounding. And he was right about his taste in movies, she thought, running her fingers along the videotape spines. He liked the blood-and-guts sort of stuff. Yuck. It was a rather impersonal place, serviceable, but a man's home, lacking in anything soft or frivolous. It was as if he'd stripped his ex-wife from the interior. Even in the kitchen.

"Foraging?"

She flinched, whirling around to face him. "No, snooping."

Her gaze shot instantly to the towel wrapped around his hips and, more important, to the bulge between his thighs.

Her cheeks reddened. "Chase, put some clothes on, for heaven's sake."

"No." Belligerent, with a teasing smile. He stood just outside the kitchen door, toweling his hair dry.

She turned away. "Please." Before I rip off that towel, she thought.

"Scare you?" he said, suddenly close to her ear.

She closed her eyes and took a shaky breath. "Hardly."

"Excite you?" he asked hopefully. She felt his fingers brush stray hairs off her neck, his breath replacing his touch. He was naked behind her. His mouth pressed to her throat, and all Tessa could think was how erotic he looked in that towel, droplets of water on his chest, the trail of hair marking a path down his stomach to the edge of green terry cloth. The goody line, her sister used to call it.

"Chase?"

"Humm?"

His arms slipped around her from behind, his hands gliding down over her tummy, caressing her thighs, fingertips dipping precariously between, then sliding up like a drape of warm velvet over her skin. She pressed back into him, his warmth. His arousal pushed and she squeezed her eyes tightly shut, covering his hands with her own as they swept up to cup her breasts. His touch was gentle and tender, but her body begged for the strength of his passion.

"I remember what you feel like, angel." His thumbs brushed her nipples. "What you smell like."

She turned in his arms, cupping his jaw and covering his mouth with hers.

Chase moaned, twisting to brace himself against the counter. He needed the support. She was coming apart on him and he pushed his knee between her legs, urging her closer. Her breathing hastened, and she sank her fingers into his hair, stroked them over his shoulders. Her urgent whimpers were driving him over the edge and when she slid her hands down to caress his nipples, Chase wanted to devour her whole.

Tessa loved the dusting of hair roughening beneath her fingertips, rubbing against her legs, and when his muscles flinched to her touch as she grazed his ribs, she couldn't resist teasing him again.

"Tessa, oh God." His mouth covered hers again, rolling and lush, his hardness warm and insistent between them. His hands, callused and heavy, moved beneath her shirt, and when hers mapped a path to his hip, dangerously close to the heat of him, Tessa drew back to look in his eyes.

His expression was laced with anticipation and she was screwing up her nerve to pull the towel away when her stomach growled rudely.

He blinked, looking down at her tummy as it voiced its emptiness again.

She dropped her forehead to his chest, her shoulders shaking with a soft chuckle. Chase laughed on a deep breath, rubbing her back, and when she tilted her head he saw apprehension in her gaze, a flicker of relief. He gritted his teeth and set her from him.

He looked down at the tenting of his towel and laughed. "A regular state around you, you know."

Tessa's mouth quivered with a smile and she tried to keep her gaze elsewhere but it wouldn't obey. "Oh my, my, my," she marveled, and this time Chase blushed. "I'm so sorry."

"No, you're not," he said, not unkindly.

He was right. It did something wonderful to her ego to know he was *that* aroused after one kiss.

"I'll feed you two in a minute. First I need another shower."

She sank back against the counter, swallowing repeatedly, then searched the cabinets for a glass, filling it to the rim and draining it. She was sitting on the sofa, her feet propped up, when he returned, damp and dressed, a suggestive smile on his lips.

He offered his hand, pulling her from the sofa and into his arms. "Come on. I have to get you out of here and at least a mile from a bed, or I'll do my best to start that," he nodded to the kitchen, "again."

Tessa felt a hot wave of desire spirit through her and deep inside she knew that there was more than just her good sense holding her back. She didn't really want this man to get his first look at her naked, while she was six months pregnant.

Chase felt it. The sexual tension. It spread like a thick blanket around them, as if the moments shared in his kitchen were relived every time they looked at or touched each other. Nothing seemed to penetrate the heavy fog of memory. It was two days since that encounter and Chase felt like a wild animal near Tessa. Her scent, the way she looked at him as if she knew his thoughts, kept pressing the image of her responses into his brain like a tape on continuous replay. Her hair, twisted in a soft chignon, begged to be let down, spread across his pillow. Her taut body, scented with cinnamon and always clothed in something feminine and seductive, tormented him, her every gesture and nuance rich with sensuality.

She had no idea how crazy she made him.

Now, in the Lamaze class, of all places, Chase could hardly control his hands, accidentally brushing her breast and aching to feel her bare skin beneath his palm, his lips. He massaged a cramp from her thigh and imagined them wrapped around him, their softness sliding luxuriously against his legs. Her secret smiles were torture, and later, as they drove to her house from the community center, Chase could think of nothing but holding her in his arms. All night.

And when she opened her door and turned to him, any gallant notion he harbored vanished and he pulled her tightly to him, kissing her till her knees softened.

"Chase. Please." She pulled back, breathless.

"Please what? Please leave?" he whispered in her ear. "Please stay?"

"I don't know," she cried against his mouth, hooking the waistband of his jeans and tugging him into her house. He shut the door, falling back against it, and kissed her again and again, his hands skating roughly down her back, over her trim hips to cup her bottom. The hard press of his thighs meshed to hers like the scrape of rough wool, driving hunger to the surface, and she whimpered against his mouth, straining to get closer. She couldn't.

"I...I can't do this," she said, pushing herself out of his arms.

"Tessa?" He caught her back and held her. "We won't do anything you don't want. A few more cold showers aren't going to hurt me."

"I know and I'm sorry. I feel like a tease, if you can believe that."

He pushed his fingers into her hair, dislodging hairpins,

his palms framing her face. "I want you, Tessa. *You.* I want to taste your breasts," he said into her mouth. "I want to feel your legs holding me, your mouth on me." His voice lowered to a husky pitch. "I want to feel you grow hot and wet before you take me inside you."

A strangled sound worked in her throat, her breathing labored. "You're not being fair."

"Do you want me, Tessa? If you say no, I'll leave, but I'll know it's a lie."

She gazed into his cobalt blue eyes. "So will I."

He kissed her lids closed and felt her sigh feather across his skin. "That's all that matters. No, don't talk. Just feel for once. I won't hurt you," he said advancing. "I swear, angel."

His mouth covered hers, the passion rising like oil to the surface. Her mouth pushed harder to his, her hands sweeping his jacket off his shoulders to the floor. The simple disrobing was an offer of trust, and Chase swore he'd move carefully. Prayed he could. He wanted her so badly. Needed her too much. He back-stepped, tugging her across the living room and down the hall, his mouth rolling over hers. He knew which room was hers without looking, the scent of her, of cinnamon and spice, drew him there.

Pulling her inside, he kissed her a moment longer before she switched on a small lamp. Chase looked at the room caught in the soft yellow glow and his jaw dropped. He should have known. A four-poster canopy bed, draped in deep mauve silks, curtained with netting and yards of fabric dramatically entwined around the posters and canopy. It was a bed made for loving Tessa.

He looked at her and she smiled shyly. And as he wondered what other secrets he'd discover this night, she started for the bathroom. He caught her hand.

"I need a minute," she said, and he let her go. Chase brushed back the curtain of the bed, securing it on the hook fashioned in the post and thought he'd bust down the door if she didn't come out soon. Then she did.

She was wrapped in a dark maroon satin robe, the outline

of her body enticingly clear. She was bare beneath. He met her gaze and saw the apprehension there and wondered if it mirrored his own. He suddenly felt inadequate.

"I haven't been with a woman since Janis," he said suddenly.

She blinked. That had to be nearly eighteen months because Janis had been dead almost a year.

"When we decided on surrogates, she felt, I guess, that the prospect of fatherhood would take care of my—needs." Bitterness tinted his tone, an embarrassed flush creeping up his neck.

A little smile curved her lips, swollen red from his kisses. "And did it?"

"Not then." He chuckled shortly, remembering the nights he'd spent just imagining being with her, so aroused he couldn't think or sleep. Then there were the cold showers, he thought with a velvety look down her body. "And definitely not now." When she wouldn't take his offered hand, he frowned softly.

After a few false starts she said, "I feel very unsexy right now."

He came to her, gathering her in his arms, his mouth brushing over her lids, her cheeks, then covering hers. He didn't offer words, for they wouldn't convince her she was the sexiest creature alive. So Chase showed her.

He kissed her throat, his hands stroking her body, fingertips dipping and brushing in every curve till she arched against him, till she responded with touches of her own. She caught his belt buckle, flipping it open, and his hands shimmered over her hair, her shoulders, as she pulled his T-shirt from his jeans with seductive care. She peeled it off over his head, her mouth immediately covering his nipple, her tongue circling the flat coin before she brought her mouth to his.

Then he realized she was shaking.

Turning her toward the cheval mirror in the corner, he stood behind her. She wouldn't look at herself, and he kissed the back of her neck and loosened the sash.

"I'd rather we did this in the dark," she said truthfully.

"I want to see you."

"Chase," she moaned weakly, and he tipped her head, taking her mouth in a deep kiss as he brushed the robe open, enfolding her breasts. She sagged back against him, covering his hands as he caressed her nipples.

He broke the kiss, looking in the mirror, a strange smile curving his mouth, and Tessa forced her gaze to the glass. His hands were a dark and rugged contrast against her skin, bronze to pale cream as they moved over her breasts, her belly.

Tessa saw the look in his eyes, in his expression. Fascination. Desire.

"You are so beautiful," he whispered in her ear, watching his hands as they moved below his child, slid to her thighs, molding them, then his fingers brushed the warmth of her womanhood. "Look at you, angel."

She was bare to his eyes and Chase drank his fill of her plush body, trim but for the roundness of life in her. Her skin was flawless, golden and creamy. He cradled the dark curls between her thighs, and stroked her lightly, loving her eager thrusts for his touch. She dampened for him and his fingers slid deeper. Her breath went ragged. His mouth trailed over her bare shoulder, her back, a grinding path down the delicate curve of her spine. Gripping her hips, he closed his eyes and tasted the softness of her buttocks, the backs of her thighs, worshipping her skin, the taste of her. She closed her hands over his and held on. Then he turned her to face him, looking up, and their eyes met and held as his rough cheek brushed softly against her belly, the curving side. Slowly he straightened, kissing her mouth before ducking his head to take her taut nipple between his lips.

She inhaled sharply, gripping his shoulders as he laved and suckled, then tasted its mate, her bosom swelling and aching for more. He drew her to the bed, sitting on the edge and pulling her to his lap. Draping her over his arm, Chase kissed her, feeling her body soften, curl toward him. He knew she was scared, knew she was uncomfortable

about him seeing her like this, but Chase realized he loved
her. Loved the woman she was, with or without their child
inside her. He wanted to make her feel as beautiful as he
saw her and he let his hand glide from her hip to the arch
of her dainty foot, slow and methodical. He palmed her
breast, shaping its weight. Then he tasted its lushness again.

His touch pierced her skin like blunt daggers, the sensation hot and heavy, and Tessa thought she'd melt into
the mattress when he took her nipple deeper into the hot
suck of his mouth. He rolled it on his tongue, and she felt
it burn with a heat that seared around her waist and drove
an ache deep between her thighs. She wanted him more.

"You'll tell me if I hurt you," he said huskily. And she
could only nod.

"Again Chase, taste me, please." And he did, his mouth
devouring her as he laid her gently on the bed, his body
nestled tightly to her side. He draped her thigh over his,
spreading her. His hand skimmed her thigh to the dark cleft
between and he rested his hand there. He rubbed. He felt
her need quicken, in her kiss, in her fingers digging into
his shoulders, and when Chase pushed two fingers inside
her, she gasped softly, her hips rising to the motion, her lip
caught between her teeth. And Chase had never seen anything so elegant as Tessa's passion.

She felt like spun glass in his arms, shimmering as his
thumb brushed the tight bead of her sex. She clung to him.
Her body pulsed heavily, sensations pulling her from all
edges and wrapping her tightly to the hand moving within
her body.

"Show it to me again, angel. Show me." She opened
her eyes and cupped his face in her palms, and Chase's
fingers pushed and withdrew until he watched the explosion
unfold in her eyes, mirrored through her body.

"Oh, Chase," she choked almost desperately, stunned as
the waves of pleasure slid over her like the pour of liquid
silver, again and again. He stroked deeply and she con-
vulsed, her breath a fractured rush of pleasure against his

lips. He held her tightly, slowing his movements till the last of her desire was spent.

Her tongue moistened her lips and she looked into his eyes.

He smiled softly, enormously pleased. "Will you explode like that with me inside you, angel?" He dipped his head, teasing her nipple with his tongue. Air rushed into her lungs. "So beautiful," he murmured and paid homage to her breast.

Her fingers sank into his hair, her eyes drifting closed.

It was a long, contented moment before he left the bed and she scooted to the center, watching him kick off his shoes, strip his socks. His fingers hovered at the band of his pants, his gaze on her as he shoved down the zipper and peeled off his briefs and jeans. Tessa absorbed the naked sight of him, his flat stomach, his muscular thighs. He was in fabulous shape, and she caught a glimpse of his taut behind in the mirror. Then her gaze lowered to his arousal, thick and proud. She swallowed, drawing the robe over her breasts.

He knelt on the bed, catching her hands in either of his. "Don't hide from me, Tessa," he said, drawing her to her knees. "Just to look at you is a turn-on. That you hold our baby inside you makes loving you more precious."

She wanted desperately to believe him, needed to believe that he wanted her for more than their child, and she pushed aside her doubts as he came closer, sliding to his back and drawing her over him. She spread her thighs, his arousal high and pulsing between them, a breath away, and she felt his incredible heat, saw his hunger.

Half propped on mounds of pillows, he watched his hands move over her breasts, her belly.

And he trembled.

Tessa knew he was restraining himself, felt it in every kiss and touch. He quaked with it. She wanted that energy, that fire they breathed into each other. He was afraid he'd hurt her, and Tessa wanted to show Chase she wasn't so fragile. She leaned over him, her tongue outlining his lips, a slow, silky motion that drove a dark burning through his bloodstream.

"Come to me, Chase," she whispered into his wet mouth. He sat up, jerking her knees around his hips, drawing her closer. And his eagerness made her laugh. She tortured him, rocking, her womanhood sliding wetly across his arousal, and he thrust against the invitation, throbbing for her. She never ceased kissing him, her mouth moving over his face, her teeth lightly scoring the curve of his jaw.

"Tessa, ah, angel." His hands dipped over her hair, her shoulders, to grip her waist.

Her tongue circled his ear and boldly she told him, "I want you inside me." She pressed tighter to him, bodies meshing, dampening. He was hot and hard, and just to be this close, naked and eager for each other, aroused her with a fierceness that scared her. Yet he wasn't hungry enough, hot enough, she thought with satisfaction and she wrapped her hand around him, enveloping him in sensations, and he slammed his eyes shut, falling back, his head digging into the pillows.

"Oh, Tessa."

Her fingers slicked over the smooth tip, drawing more moisture, and he came unglued, twisting beneath her. His hands on her thighs tightened and flexed. A groan close to pain rumbled in his wide chest. She stroked him again, mercilessly, and Chase knew if he allowed her to continue, he'd be useless any second. He pried her hand from him.

"Now you're teasing me," he murmured, burying his face in the curve of her throat, his hand riding her spine. He chuckled shakily. "Don't stop."

"I can't wait, Chase. Now, now." She rose slightly, guiding him inside her.

"Careful," he warned, looking into her soft green eyes, but she could tell he wanted nothing more than to toss her on her back and ravish her. The thought made her skin sizzle.

He laced his fingers with hers, his arms braced back against the mattress, and he gave her balance and power.

He was tight within her and she lifted, then slid downward, encasing him slowly, her body adjusting and squeezing him.

"You're like a rock," she gasped on a laugh, and a tiny smile curved his mouth. Chase thrust his hips gently to greet her. Sweat dampened their bodies, her hips catching cadence and taking him with her as he sat up and filled her deeper.

His breathing labored, he caressed her breasts, her belly tight with the pull of desire, then clasped her hips, riding the motion. She held his gaze, her fingers digging into his shoulders, her breath rasping into his mouth. She was liquid passion, her body slick and sliding, and Chase let her have total control. She pushed, faster, harder, curling into him, and he felt her release, experienced the pinpricking sensation shooting through her and into him.

"Chase, Chase!"

He arched, his arousal throbbing, his strong hands grinding her tightly to his groin as he erupted inside her. Her muscles flexed and gripped and Chase felt every tiny quiver as he held her snugly, raining kisses over her face and hair till the last tremor faded.

His hand trembled as he brushed damp tresses back to look into her eyes. "I'm in love with you, Tessa Lightfoot."

Something broke inside Tessa then and her eyes burned. "I know." She flung her arms around his neck, burying her face in the curve of his throat. "I know."

He didn't mistake the hopelessness in her voice. He rubbed her back in soothing circles before he eased her down to the bed. She kissed him liquidly as he tossed a cover over her and she snuggled in his arms, drifting quickly into sleep.

But Chase couldn't rest. He stared at the canopy and felt electrified. He wanted to wake her and make love to her again. He'd never known anything like being with this

woman, inside her, held by her. She was sexy and passion-
ate and he wanted her to be his wife. But her reaction to
his claim left him wounded and confused. It seemed, he
thought, that it was going to take a lot more than words to
convince Tessa that he loved her first.

Nine

Tessa was having a delicious dream, her body awake and aroused, yet her mind lethargic. She reached for Chase, yet when she found the space beside her empty, she succumbed to the dream, enjoying the erotic sensations curling through her like smoke. Vaguely she felt a warmth against her thigh.

"Chase," she whispered, yet refused to open her eyes, afraid the dream would end. Between her thighs was damp and hot, and she tried to close them, to ease the ache, but couldn't. Suddenly she was fully awake and aware.

"What are you doing?"

"Tasting you," he said without hesitation.

Her face burned and she flung her arm over her eyes. "Oh please, don't stop now!"

He didn't, his tongue laving at the core of her. Instinctively she drew her leg up and Chase eased two fingers inside her.

"I'd rather have you," she whispered into the darkened room. He climbed onto the bed beside her, tucking her to the curve of his body, her back to his chest. Effortlessly, he entered her.

She moaned deliciously. "Are you always this insatiable?"

"Only with you, angel." He withdrew and surged deeply. "Devious of me, wasn't it?"

"Yes. Oh, heavens!" Tessa felt every glorious inch of him penetrate her and she clutched a pillow, biting it to keep from moaning like a banshee.

"I want to drive into you," he whispered in a husky voice, his arms wrapped around her as he withdrew and slid slowly home. "I want to make love with you every way imaginable and I never want to stop."

"Me, too," she whispered, then twisted a look at him. "Me, too."

His expression was pleased, strained and sharp with his fountaining need, and she touched his cheek.

"Chase," she gasped, feeling her release approach with the force of a flood, a flood she wanted him to join, and she leaned back into him, flinging one leg brazenly back over his muscled thigh.

And he touched where the air touched her body, stroking her tender bud and feeling her slide into heaven. The warmth of the room buffeted her cries, her straining whimpers as he pushed and pushed and she took him, squeezing the life from him, feminine muscles flexing and clenching with their power.

In a soft burst of needed air, they collapsed deeper into the down covers.

"They have names for men like you, Chase Madison," she muttered into her pillow, then glared at him.

He grinned, unashamed of his tactics. "I wanted to wake you an hour ago."

"Try to contain yourself for at least another two hours," she said, patting his thigh and snuggling into the cocoon of his warmth.

Chase watched her sleep, her breathing even, and he brushed a strand of black hair from her cheek. He pressed his lips there. "I love you, Tessa," he whispered on a shaky breath.

Tessa wasn't asleep and her heart jumped every time he said it, but logic and reason interfered, tainting the sweet proclamation. Did he really love her or was it his feeling for his child speaking? Tormented that she might never know the answer, she followed the disturbing thoughts into the arms of sleep.

Her body spooned with his, Chase slipped his arm around her, her breast filling his palm. She snuggled closer, a tangle of arms and legs and wrinkled sheets. Light crept across the mauve carpet when Chase finally found the peace of dreams, Tessa wrapped in his arms and his heart in her hands. Falling in love with her was dangerous, he realized, because now she had the power to destroy him with a few simple words.

Tessa woke slowly, her body sated, and she stretched languidly, reaching for the man beside her. Her hand met emptiness and she shifted to her side and smiled. Rose petals lay strewn over the depression his body had left. She scooped up a handful and inhaled their fragrance. A note slid off the pillow.

Get up, lazy. Be back at nine with breakfast.

She glanced at the clock and scrambled off the bed and into a quick shower. Sitting on the couch, she was dressed and mildly awake when Chase came through the front door. His khaki slacks and blue polo shirt told her he'd stopped by his place. She flung the newspaper aside and drew her knees up, patting the space on the sofa beside her. Chase bent and kissed her forehead, then emptied the bag onto the table.

"Good God, Chase. Who did you invite?" There was enough food to feed a small country.

He sat. "I wasn't sure what you wanted, and I'm starved." He wiggled his brows suggestively, in case she forgot why.

"Nice to know I can work a man into starvation," she

said, sinking back into the overstuffed cushions, sliding her feet behind him. "Now what did you bring for yourself?" He chuckled, unwrapping food, and her gaze slipped over him, the shirt straining against his arms, his trim hips. She remembered last night, the long slope of his naked thighs between hers, counting the ridges in his stomach as he dozed, then watching him thicken with desire as she smoothed her hand over his taut body. He enjoyed her touch and that made her want to do it more, to feel him squirm and beg. It was a power she had never known before. In a heartbeat she knew she could make love with him again. Right here.

She let her bare foot slide over his waist, teasing his ribs, his back, and he turned, his look sly and aware of her intent.

Bracing his hand on the back of the sofa, he loomed over her, his face nearing. Her hands pressed to his chest, molding up across his strength before wrapping around his neck. His mouth was heavy on hers, his tongue pushing between her parted lips, sweeping lazily inside, and she was noticeably breathless and flushed when he drew back.

"Morning, angel."

She found her breath and swallowed. It really was unfair, the way he could make her all hot and bothered with just a kiss.

"Good morning." She pushed a lock of dark brown hair back off his forehead.

His frown was soft. "How do you feel?"

"Like a woman who's had really great sex."

He went very still. "Was that all it was?"

She traced the lines in his features, smoothing them out. "You know better than to ask that, Chase."

His throat bobbed. "Do I?"

Her brows knitted. She'd never seen him unsure. It made him more vulnerable, and Tessa's heart ached for him.

"I love you, Chase."

He blinked. "Really? Ah, I mean…really?" The hope in his voice quivered through her, stealing her breath and bringing tears to her eyes.

"You're kind of hard not to love, handsome."

"Aha, found out," he said, bussing her lips, her cheeks, his heart thundering wildly. "I've spent my life trying to get every pregnant woman I see to love me." He swallowed thickly. "But you're the first to fall."

His voice trembled as he spoke, and Tessa pulled him to the sofa beside her.

"I love you, but I won't marry you." He tried to sit up, but she held him down, his head pillowed on her shoulder, his hand on her tummy. "I won't marry you because I can't escape the feelings I have that you're asking because you're our baby's father. No, please don't say anything yet," she asked when he tried to look at her. "Let me get this out. It's unfair to you, since you seem so sure of yourself, but I have to think of this child first, Chase. Is it best for her if we go into a marriage with misgivings and doubts that haunt—every minute?"

She stroked his hair lovingly and closed her eyes. She was hurting him and she hated herself for it. But she'd failed at marriage before with Ryan, because of a baby she never had. And with her child, *their* child connecting her and Chase before their feelings ever did, she was scared of making another mistake and ruining Chase's life just because it *seemed* the best thing to do for the child. She'd never know if it was her or his child he wanted. And watching her own mother suffer over the same situation made her think more than twice about whom they'd affect later on.

"I love you, Chase. So very much." She brushed her mouth over his soft, shiny hair, her words warm against his head. "But I don't trust either of us right now enough to make a decision that will alter all our lives forever." Her breath shuddered. "Please try to understand."

"I'm trying." But he wanted to shake her. His child moved restlessly inside her and Chase sympathized. He felt confined, playing by her rules, but as her tears wet his hair, he decided that he'd wait her out. And if she still refused, he'd bring in the big guns. But he was going to marry Tessa. He'd die without her.

Six weeks later Chase stood beside Tessa's design table, admiring the sketches, a wedding dress, a little girl's party outfit. But tucked in the corner of the wide table was a scrap torn from a magazine: a baby's room. He studied it, smiling. Even if she didn't want the stuff he'd given her in the baby's room, she knew what she wanted.

The doorbell sounded.

"Would you get that?" Tessa called from the kitchen.

He inhaled the delicious smells pouring through the house, then crossed to the door. He flung it open and stared at the woman on Tessa's doorstep.

"You must be Chase," she said, inspecting him critically from head to toe.

"And you are?"

She put up a hand, a truckload of silver bracelets racking her wrist, then stepped forward and grabbed his hand, pushing her way inside and staring intensely at his palm. Tessa poked her head out of the kitchen and sighed, shaking her head.

"Angel?" he said, helpless.

"I see you've met Mom."

He glanced sideways at the woman. "Not exactly."

Tessa's mother was oblivious to the conversation and Tessa's look begged him to have patience. Some of her family were apparently a little outside of the loop.

Chase studied the woman. Tessa had her features, soft, angelically smooth, but her mother's hair was red, flame red and wild with curls. Her slender body was clothed in silks with an uneven, tattered look in shades of blue and purple. A ring circled every finger, and Chase resisted the urge to inspect her toes.

"Mom?"

Celeste looked up after a moment and smiled. She patted his hand and Chase took it back, shoving both hands into the pockets of his cutoffs and wishing he were dressed a little better.

"Tessa, darling, look at you," her mother crooned dramatically, grasping her hands and stretching her arms wide to get a decent look at her nearly eight-month tummy. Bracelets jangled and a huge tapestry handbag swung from her arm. Her mom's eyes teared. "Oh, you're just... just—"

"Pleasingly plump?" Tessa ventured when she thought her mother would cry.

Celeste laughed, a soft husky sound, and Chase knew where he'd heard it before: from Tessa, in bed.

Tessa closed her arms around her mother, savoring the warm hug, and winked at Chase over her shoulder. Celeste Lightfoot was a tiny thing.

"We were just about to have lunch."

"No red meat, I hope. Nitrates, you know."

Chase flung his arm around Tessa, pressing his lips to her temple to smother a snicker. If Celeste only knew how Tessa had devoured an inch-thick T-bone steak last night, she'd be horrified.

"Grilled chicken. Come on." She grabbed her mother's hand and the two women headed toward the kitchen.

"Chase," Tessa called when he wasn't right behind her. She popped her head out of the kitchen, motioning wildly for him to join them, looking almost panicked.

Chase gestured to the door, inching toward it. "Ahh, I have a couple errands—"

Tessa moved across the floor with more speed than he thought possible. "Do I have to bribe you?"

He swept one arm around her, settling his hand familiarly on the curve of her bottom. "What did you have in mind?" His brows wiggled, his hand squeezing.

"Chase!" she hissed, giving him a shove, aware of exactly where his mind was right then.

Her blush made him chuckle softly.

Tessa gave a furtive glance toward the kitchen. "She'll

be inventorying my cupboards and tossing anything that isn't organically grown out the window, you'll see.''

"Not my peanut butter cookies!" he said in mock horror.

She ribbed him. ''If you hurry you might save them from total annihilation.''

Urging her toward the kitchen, Chase inhaled deeply, mentally preparing himself for an afternoon with a woman he hoped would soon be his mother-in-law.

Two hours later, Chase and Celeste were relaxing on the back porch, drinking some horrific tea Celeste had prepared herself. She'd pumped him full of herbs, insisting he consumed too many nitrates, and that the tea should purify his system. Chase, not wanting to offend her, took them only after Tessa discreetly assured him he would not turn into a mutant. He smacked his lips, tasting grass and feeling like a well-grazed cow.

Tessa napped inside and Chase wanted to join her. Celeste Lightfoot was tiring on a man and he felt a pang of sympathy for Tessa's father, Walter. He'd probably died from Celeste exposure. She chatted nonstop, couldn't seem to be still, and her bracelets jangled with every gesture. But Chase liked her. She had a special energy, a oneness with the universe, as she chose to see it. And she loved her daughters.

"You're sleeping together, aren't you?"

He'd grown accustomed to her bluntness in the past hour or so. Chase nodded.

"Good."

His brows shot up. Hardly the reaction he'd expected.

"Tessa needs to feel like a woman right now. I know from experience that the bigger you get, the less attractive you feel, and you just want it over with.''

"I think she's beautiful. I love her."

She reached out and patted his hand. ''I know, Chase, honey. I know. And you've been patient, but it'll take a lot more to handle my Tessa.''

His forehead wrinkled. ''I don't want to handle her, Celeste.''

Celeste scoffed, finished off her tea, then threw her legs over the side of the chaise lounge chair. She stared across the small separation at Chase. "I didn't want her to get pregnant that way. Nothing anyone could say would change her mind. She's stubborn." Chase smiled. *That* he knew. "No, understand. Even when the doctors said it was risky and could be painful, she charged ahead." Celeste shook her head and Chase sat up a bit straighter. "When I think how Dia made her life miserable, constantly offering unwanted legal advice and whatnot." Celeste broke her gaze, and Chase imagined he saw a flicker of guilt in her bright green eyes. She seemed to struggle with her words and when she spoke, Chase felt it wasn't what she really wanted to say. "If she doesn't want to marry you, Chase, it will be hard to change her mind."

Her tone implied hope, and Chase smiled. "Let me worry about it, Celeste."

"I will," she said as if she'd imagined no other prospect. She nodded, flinging long red curls off her shoulder before she stood. Chase rose, and after Celeste had peeked in on Tessa, sleeping like a wrecked train, he walked her to the door. "It'll work out in the end," she said, patting his hand, but her eyes said there would be a lot of pain in getting there.

"She gone?"

He whirled and found Tessa peering around the corner.

"You little sneak."

"Mom tends to be a bit—"

He peered. "Zealous?"

She laughed softly, leaning against the wall as he came to her. Her body heated at the sight of him, lean and tan in cutoffs and a black tank top. And she slid her arms around his waist, envious of its trimness.

"She doesn't think you'll marry me."

"She's right."

He frowned, the scowl masking his hurt. "I swear I don't understand you, angel. I love you. You love me. Why not?"

Uncertainty. Was she feeling this way because he was her baby's father or was it because she'd finally found true, honest love? The uncertainty was eating at her. And then there was the fear. She kept remembering her mother and father, the arguments, the nights her mom spent sobbing when she thought none of her daughters could hear. She couldn't do that to her own child. But the uncertainty wore on her the hardest. "I just can't."

"I'll keep asking." He said it like a warning and she brushed her mouth across his.

"I know. You're annoying like that, but I love you anyway."

His smile was easy, but it didn't quite reach his eyes this time. Loving Tessa was almost a challenge of wills. Her will. He *was* happy. He adored her, God knew. But a man had only so much patience to stretch. And he wondered when and what would make his snap.

A couple weeks later, Chase helped Tessa into the car. She looked exhausted, her hair slipping from the knot on her crown, dark smudges under her eyes. A stab of sympathy bent through him. She was less than three weeks away from her due date and she was miserable. She hadn't slept well lately, couldn't get comfortable no matter how many pillows she propped under and around her. During the times he did stay the night, it was like fending off a rampaging sea of stuffed animals to get to her.

"Maybe you should close the shop for a couple...of days...a week." His words trailed off at the deadly glare she sent him.

"Stuff it, Chase. I'm not closing until I have to."

His features tightened. Her obstinance was no longer amusing, and he wanted to shake her. "Be reasonable, Tessa. Look at your feet, for God's sake!"

"I know what they look like. *I* feel it!"

He reared back and she stared out the windshield, regretting her waspish mood when he was only trying to be helpful. Chase moved around the Jeep and climbed behind the wheel.

Tessa hated that she was so big he had to drive her everywhere, hated that she had to depend on *anyone* just to do the simplest things, and Tessa knew, *she knew,* it wasn't his fault.

"I'm sorry," she said when he closed the door.

"I love you."

She lifted her gaze to his, her lips trembling as she waved him closer. Cupping his strong jaw, she stared into his blue eyes. "I love you too, darling. Don't forget that."

"Even when you rip into me like a wounded tiger?"

She kissed him then, silencing and warm, then smoothed her thumb over his lips. "Always."

He settled back into the seat and drove her home. The ride was painfully quiet.

"Do you mind if I don't ask you to stay?" she said at the door, and his expression froze on his face. "I'm just so tired."

"I'll miss you." He brushed a kiss over her soft mouth. "Rest. I'll see you tomorrow." She kissed him once more, then slipped inside.

It wasn't like they spent every night together, he reasoned, trying not to feel hurt. He wished she'd share with him whatever was really bothering her.

The next day, Tessa braced her hand at the base of her spine, massaging the ache, and stared out her shop window. Business was slow and she was grateful for the reprieve. Her legs and feet were killing her. She was as big as a house and she decided that being pregnant was only fun until the seventh month; then it was like a bothersome stone strapped to her middle. She swore if someone told her how wonderfully round and radiant she looked, she'd deck them and like it. Rubbing her back, she walked to the rear of the store. Dana smiled wanly and Tessa apologized for snapping at her earlier, then went to sort through sizes and collect discarded garments. She blamed hormones, the extra weight, the throbbing in her back or the pressure that wouldn't let her sleep, but really she wanted to blame Chase.

Yet she couldn't. God, she couldn't so much as move without him coming to her rescue, always attentive, smiling so much there were times she wanted to smack it off his face. And now that she was so close to delivering what she felt was a female version of Big Foot, they couldn't make love. It was just as well. She had no desire, felt too fat and awkward. But she missed the intimacy. It was something tangible to cling to when she felt her emotions get the better of her.

She couldn't ask for a better man and she loved Chase so much it hurt to look in his eyes and say no when he proposed, which he did every morning, swearing one day he'd wear her down till she agreed. Saying no was wearing on her just as much as asking was on him. But she couldn't marry him and she had tried for days to examine her feelings. All she found were doubts and fears, fears that he loved her *because* of their baby; that when their child was born, he'd lose interest; that she could never trust her heart or his words. The only way she could protect herself was to cling to her independence. To give it up would be like removing a protective cloak. If she married him, she'd never know if this was for real and everlasting. Or for the baby. *And how will you know anyway?* a voice pestered. *The baby will always be there.* Tears threatened and Tessa swallowed. I'm such a mess, she thought dismally.

"Excuse me? Tessa?"

Tessa flinched, so deep in her thoughts she didn't hear the door chime. She turned and found a sharply dressed woman in her late fifties. "May I help you?" Tessa frowned softly, then her features stretched tight. "Mrs. Madison," she realized. The picture in Chase's place. She was the woman who'd shopped here the day Chase waited on Lila Dewberry.

"Come sit down, dear. I'm exhausted just watching you

move around,'' she said efficiently, and Tessa joined her on the small Queen Anne settee tucked against the wall.

She was suddenly nervous.

"I'm Carole Anne.'' She held out her hand and Tessa grasped it.

Carole Anne noticed her cold hand trembled and rubbed it gently, her expression laced with so much compassion, Tessa felt her composure slip. "I know.''

"Oh, Tessa,'' she said softly. "I haven't come to badger you, if that's what you think." Tessa admitted she did. "Chase didn't send me here.''

Tessa blinked.

"Carl and I were hoping you'd come visit, but when you didn't—" she shrugged "—we understood.''

"I wish I did,'' Tessa said sullenly.

Chase's mother scooted closer. "You aren't in this alone, Tessa. Nothing has to be done now. I know my son. He loves with everything he has. Yet he can be very persistent.'' Tessa smiled at that solid intuition. "But if it doesn't work out between you, I want you to know there is a place for you and your baby in our lives.'' She hesitated. "If you'll have us.''

Tessa's eyes watered. "I won't deny you your grandchild, Carole Anne, but that isn't the problem. I love Chase. I do,'' she cried softly. "But I can't seem to trust it, to just let go like he wants. Not when I feel like this.'' She gestured to her stomach.

"Perhaps putting your feelings aside till after the baby comes is best, then?''

Tessa shrugged, staring at the floor and wishing she could see her feet. "Wish I could, but putting a hold on loving him just isn't possible.''

Carole Anne smiled, pleased, but Tessa didn't see it. "Then perhaps seeing less of each other might help?''

A sound worked in her throat. The thought of a day passing without seeing Chase squeezed down on her heart. But what Carole Anne said was reasonable, and Tessa decided that's where Chase had inherited the trait. Until this child was born, they couldn't decide anything, and Tessa knew she was in no frame of mind right now.

"Mom? What are you doing here?"

Both women looked up and Chase's gaze shot between them, ending on Tessa. "Are you okay, angel?"

She nodded and he moved closer, giving his mother a stay-out-of-this look. Carole Anne stood, catching her eldest son's arm in a gentle but firm grasp, and Chase suddenly felt ten years old from the assessing look in her eyes.

"Patience, Chase. And remember our little chat," she ended in warning.

She brushed a kiss to Tessa's cheek, told her to call if she wanted to talk, then left the shop with all the class of a sloop in full sail.

He remembered his mom's *little chat.* She'd done all the talking and expected him to heed her warnings that men never have babies and can't sympathize nor understand the physical burden and the emotional upheaval women experience. That if he had any romantic notions about speaking vows moments before their child was born, he could forget it. Women were scared at this time, no matter the brave front they showed. Fear of stillbirth, handicaps, anything they could imagine might happen, fueled the prospects of impending motherhood, and men couldn't share in it. It made Chase feel cut out, and his Dad had stood by, listening, then finally agreed with his mom.

But the closer they came to her due date, the more Chase felt Tessa was pushing him away. Giving birth shouldn't have anything to do with their love, he kept telling himself. But as he looked into her face, strained and unhappy, he knew it did.

He sat down beside her, and Tessa sank into his arm, snuggling her cheek against his chest.

Chase closed his eyes and prepared himself. "You've decided something, haven't you?"

She nodded, quiet tears soaking his shirt.

"Whatever you want Tessa, I'll do it." His hand roamed familiarly over her belly. "*If* it's what *you* want."

Dread deepened his voice and Tessa didn't want to hurt him, never wanted to, but she just couldn't rely on her feelings right now. She couldn't think clearly. And although she doubted being apart would make her life simpler, she hoped she'd have a decisive bearing on their situation, maybe even erase the doubts that hovered like an ax about to fall. She was breaking his heart and draining his patience. Her emotions and logic did a constant side-stepping, giving her real contentment and love one moment, then riddling her into a pile of emotional mush the next. And it was growing harder and harder to look into his hopeful eyes each time he asked her to be his wife.

She squeezed her eyes shut, forcing the words past her pain, the agony she'd give him. "Till the baby comes, I don't think we should see each other."

Hurt stabbed through Chase, and his mouth tightened in a grim line. He was right. She *could* destroy him with just a few well-chosen words.

What she'd said didn't really hit him until later that day when he went to put on his cutoffs and realized they were at Tessa's. It made him irritable. And during the next week, he felt like a voyeur, a pervert, stealing looks at her from a distance. Seeing, but not touching. He passed her on the road and nearly smashed his Jeep, saw her in the market and felt as if she'd kicked him in the teeth when she made a complete turnaround, leaving her basket in the center aisle.

Yet he called her every day, needed to hear her voice, and though she wasn't her usual conversational self, she talked about anything except what she was feeling. Or what she was doing to him. And when he hung up the phone, he felt drained from avoiding the subject of how totally she'd pushed him out of her life.

Then, after a week, he got angry.

"You're acting too much like Christian," Colin said from across the table.

Chase's eyes shot over the poor excuse for a poker hand

as he tossed a chip onto the table. "Is that right?" Colin didn't notice the explosive edge in Chase's tone or he would have just kept his mouth shut.

"Yeah, lighten up. One depressing hermit brother is enough. Besides, Bro, it's only till the baby comes."

"Back off, Colin," Tigh said and anted up.

Colin glanced at his sixth-grade buddy and frowned, then looked at Chase. "You want to talk about it?" Colin said, waiting till he met his gaze.

"Nothing to say." Chase slapped the cards on the table, the chair scraping back as he stood. "*I* have nothing to say about it. Tessa rules, didn't you know that? Tessa says leave, butt out, and like a goddamned trained puppy, I do it!"

Colin reared back and the other men—his foreman, Dave, and another co-worker—blanched.

Tigh said nothing, staring at his cards.

Chase looked around the table at his friends, friends he'd vented his anger on in the past two weeks. It would serve him right if they beat the tar out of him. And Chase realized that's just what he wanted, a good fight. "Later," he muttered, heading to the door.

He could hardly stand himself. He'd fought with everyone around him, rode his crew as if the world would end tomorrow and, God forgive him, yelled at his mother for interfering. His dad had nearly put him through the wall for that.

Chase was furious. With Tessa for kicking him out of her life and at himself for letting her dictate their relationship. He'd been damn noble about this, he reasoned. He'd dredged up every tender feeling and scrap of sympathy to see things her way.

As he drove to her house, he planned to have it out with her.

And say what? Hurry up and have the baby so I can reason with you?

Marry me or else?

I love you so much I can't stand another moment of being apart, of not holding you and hearing your laugh?

He pulled up in front of her house, viciously shoving the gear into park, and caught a glimpse of his reflection in the rearview mirror. He looked awful, tired. If he looked this bad, how did *she* feel? He pressed his forehead to the steering wheel, closing his eyes. Don't weaken, he warned, don't compromise. Anger was the only thing he wanted to feel right now. To let anything else in would turn him into a marshmallow the instant he saw her. Suddenly he left the car, slamming the door and heading up the walk like a Marine charging an enemy camp. He rapped hard on the door, rattling the windows, then shoved his hands in his pockets, pacing. Nothing. He squinted into the windows, but the curtains were drawn. At least the lights were on, he thought, and rapped again.

Then he heard a moan.

Ten

Chase's heart jumped to his throat and he fumbled with his keys, trying to find the one for her front door. He shoved open the door and saw her, on her knees, clutching her belly. For a moment he was frozen to the ground.

She twisted a look over her shoulder, flinging her hand out to him. "Chase! Help me!"

Two strides and he slid to his knees beside her. She was breathing fast, her body sheened in sweat.

"Jesus, Tessa. How long?" He pushed damp hair off her face to look at her. "Why didn't you call me?"

"I tried," she wailed and gestured to the cellular phone a few feet away on the floor. "It started yesterday. I didn't think much of it until the pains got stronger. Johanna said it could be a while, but then my water broke—" Suddenly she bent over as a contraction ripped through her body. "Oh God," she gasped. "I've been trying to get to the phone."

"It's okay, angel," he soothed, gathering her in his arms.

"No, it's early and I can't stand!"

Chase was surprised at how calm he was when he thought he'd choke on his heart any second. Carefully he stood, cradling her against his chest. "Breathe, angel. Look at me." He paused at the door, nudging it shut. "Tessa," he called when she was panting too hard, and she lifted her bleary gaze to his. "I won't let anything hurt you."

She scoffed, wetting her lips. "I don't think you can control this."

"Want those drugs yet?"

"Yes!" she groaned as he placed her carefully in the seat of his Jeep. Chase was inside and down the road in seconds. He dialed the doctor from his car phone, plastering what he hoped resembled a smile on his face. She looked as if she'd die before he got her to the hospital. En route he auto-dialed her family and his. Inside the hospital was no less hectic, the exam divulging that she was already dilated to nine centimeters.

Chase was going to be a father in a matter of minutes.

Panic set in. He couldn't go in there, he thought numbly as a nurse helped him into scrubs and a ridiculous-looking cap. He couldn't. He swallowed, looked at the nurse and shook his head. The young woman sent him a kind smile, then propelled him through the double doors like a cop taking a prisoner. Then he heard Tessa scream his name and Chase hurried alongside the nurse as she ushered him into a room. The sight of Tessa in a birthing chair made his knees weak, and his features tightened.

Johanna nodded supportively, then tipped the chair back slightly.

"Won't be long, Tessa," she said as she examined her. "Next time though, come in earlier."

"There won't *be* a next time," she said through gritted teeth, then glared accusingly at Chase.

"Hey," he whispered in her ear. "I didn't have the pleasure of putting this one in you." But I will the next one, he thought. I will.

He looked pale, she thought with malicious pleasure, yet he coached her, got in her face, helped her breathe, bathed her forehead, offered her ice chips, and Tessa thought if she got this baby out, she'd never consider doing it again. Never.

"Slow down, angel." She was panting too fast, her skin chalky.

"Okay, Tessa. Let's get this baby born." Johanna moved between her legs and Chase thought she looked like a quarterback ready for the snap. Johanna glanced at the fetal monitor. "Breathe, breathe. Come on, Tessa, you can do this. No, don't push, not yet."

"I have to!" Her cheeks puffed with her pant-blows, her effort not to push.

"Look at me, angel." Chase wiped a cloth over her face, pushing her head back, and she lifted tired eyes. "I love you. You can do this."

"I want to," she gasped. "But I can't." She was so tired.

"It's too late for drugs," he said with a smirk, and Tessa smiled weakly, sagging into the chair as the contraction ended. Johanna nodded to Chase.

"This is it, Tessa." Panic and fear streaked across her features at the doctor's words, then she calmed, amazing him, and concentrated. Tessa focused on nothing, yet her mind filled with fractured images—of Chase pulling her onto his lap in the restaurant and smoothing her belly, of his warm, strong hands massaging her back, pointing to the tiny fingers and claiming she carried his son, of his eyes tearing when he saw the sonogram. The contraction grew stronger, a tight, downward, yanking pressure she was certain would rip her in half. She clutched his hand, crushing his fingers.

Chase grit his teeth. Any pain he suffered couldn't be near what she was going through. He watched, glancing at Johanna, oblivious to the nurses and instructions filtering around them. He stared at Tessa, loving her so deeply and praying she'd make it. She looked so helpless as she fought to push out their child.

"Push, push!" Johanna commanded. "Don't stop till I tell you."

Tessa strained, then let loose a guttural scream, of pain and triumph. Chase no longer felt his fingers, yet he watched. Watched Tessa strain. Watched his child enter the world screaming at them for disturbing his peace.

"It's a boy!" Johanna said, holding the child up for them to see. The infant shrieked and squirmed and his parents laughed.

"Told you so," he whispered, and Tessa sagged back, lifting her gaze to his. She brushed her thumb across his cheek, catching the single tear.

"You'll never let me forget that, huh?"

He shook his head, his voice lost somewhere he couldn't retrieve, and he buried his face in the curve of her throat, smoothing back her damp hair. "You did good, angel. He's beautiful. I'm so proud of you."

He kissed her softly, reverently, and Tessa felt a sharpness in her chest. She'd missed him so much these past weeks. Then their son was laid on her chest and Tessa laughed and cried. Her baby shivered.

"Ohh, it's okay," she cooed, covering her son, wiping his face. She glanced at Chase and his hand trembled as he stroked his son's head.

While Johanna finished with Tessa, a nurse carried their son to a table. Chase couldn't take his eyes off the tiny bundle, and after a few quick tests, she gestured for him to join her.

Chase gazed down at the wiggling infant, his son's movements jerky, his breathing a little noisy, and he bent, pressing his lips to the soft newborn cheek. A son. With shaking hands, Chase gave his son his first bath, counting tiny fingers and toes, softly talking to him, telling him how glad he was to finally meet him, that this better be the last time he caused his mother any pain. Then he sang, almost in a private whisper, *Happy Birthday*.

The room went suddenly quiet and Johanna glanced up, looking at Chase's back, then at Tessa. Tessa met her doctor's gaze over the mounds of sheets. She easily read Johanna's look. *Are you going to let him get away?*

A hard knot worked in her throat. Tears filled her eyes and she let them quietly fall. This was the happiest moment of her life. She had the baby she'd always wanted, needed, and his father loved them. Chase lifted his son in his arms, and when Tessa saw the awed look on his face, the unconditional love shining in his blue eyes, she knew there was nothing more heart-wrenching than the tiny speck of human enveloped in his strong hands. He carefully placed the infant in her arms.

"I think he likes me."

Tessa's lips twitched with a patient smile. He sounded uncertain and hopeful.

"Look at those hands." He caught one, spreading the fingers, his thumb covering his son's entire palm. "Baseball hands," he said almost to himself. "Maybe football."

She didn't respond, unsure. But images of a dark-haired child bent over, his hands braced on his knees, his little bottom swaying side to side like his father's always did, raced through her mind. It made her chest tighten.

The room cleared and Chase didn't notice until a nurse asked him to take his son. From behind a curtain, she helped Tessa bathe and get into clean garments and a bed. The birthing chair was wheeled out and Chase waited off in the corner, his son snuggled against his chest, seeking warmth and the comfort of his heartbeat.

He smiled at the soft mewing sound his boy made and brushed his lips across his soft, down-covered head. *Baby boy Lightfoot* read the tape on his tiny ankle, and Chase felt a measure of resentment. It should be his name there. And as he considered a majestic list of names, since they'd never discussed them, he wondered if he was going to be named on the birth certificate.

He'd fight for the right, he decided, then pushed the week's worth of anger and hurt aside as the nurse swept the curtain back. He met Tessa's gaze across the room. She was exhausted, but had never looked more beautiful. Her hair brushed, her face freshly washed, she was once again the delicate, angelic female who tore his world apart. A far cry from the raving lunatic delivering his son. Alone with her, he moved to the bed. She immediately held her arms out for their child.

"What do we call him?"

We. The single word was a burst of reality. No matter what happened, they would always be connected by their baby, she thought, adjusting the blanket around her son's cherubic face. "I've always liked Christopher, or maybe Zackary." She cast him a quick glance.

"Christopher," he said with finality, and after a moment, she nodded. "'Course, Christian will think he's named for him." His lips twisted in a rueful smile, his eyes on his son. "Maybe he'll come home to visit more often for his nephew."

Tessa's brows drew down. Except for his daily calls in the past weeks, they'd been out of touch with each other's lives, and she realized how much his family meant to him.

"You haven't been riding him again, have you?" His gaze shot to hers, his guilty flush speaking volumes. "When he's ready to face the world, he will."

He nodded, settling on the bed beside her, and a part of Chase's heart cracked when she cuddled their son protectively. He let it pass. But he felt as if he were talking to a stranger, and Chase wondered if he had imagined the past months. Did she still love him? Did she show him her passion because she only wanted to keep him happy so he wouldn't petition for custody? He hated to think that of Tessa, for she wasn't a manipulative person, but right now, Chase felt her precious love fading before his eyes.

God, he thought, his throat so tight it threatened his breathing. He couldn't hurt this much in a lifetime.

"I'm sure your family is here." He inclined his head toward the door. He didn't mention that, in all likelihood, so was his.

She nodded. "In a few minutes," she whispered against Christopher's head. "I want to be alone with my son."

Chase's expression sharpened, but he didn't comment and leaned close, smoothing his hand over his baby's back and kissing him. He met her gaze, inches from her face. "I love you, Tessa. I always will."

Then he kissed her.

A deep, sexy kiss, the kind he tortured her with when he was loving her body, smooth and hot. Tessa reacted instantly, cupping his head, pressing him closer, reminding herself that she was being foolish and reckless and risking a good man's heart with her tangled emotions. She sobbed against his mouth and he drank it, sliding his arm around her and kissing her until she was breathless, her eyes glazed.

Slowly he drew back and, without meeting her gaze, he left. Tessa looked down at her son and cried.

Chase was composed when he entered the waiting room and announced that they had a son. His mother cried, hugging him, as his father pumped his hand, his aging eyes a little misty. Celeste sobbed quietly, then popped out of her chair, bracelets jingling as she declared she *must* read her grandson's palm first thing. Colin hooted, slapped his brother on the back and passed out cigars as if he were the daddy. Yet a moment later, he was strangely silent.

Chase met Samantha, Tessa's elder sister, up close and personal for the first time and recognized the resemblance immediately. She could be Tessa's twin except for her height and dark auburn hair. There was something ethereal about her, calm in a sea of excitement, and when she wrapped her arms around him, she whispered, "She's being a stubborn brat again, isn't she?"

Chase chuckled mirthlessly and nodded.

"Be stubborn back, then," she said.

He liked her already and tried to recall Tessa's reasons for insisting that her sister was "out there on another plane of existence."

"Some people need rescuing from themselves, Chase," she added, before leaving his arms.

Her gaze shifted to Christian, who was staring out the window, and as if he suspected her eyes were on him, he slowly turned his head. His brows rose, his gaze pinning Samantha briefly before she dragged her eyes back to Chase. She patted his hand, much like Celeste, and pressed a chunk of crystal into his palm.

"This will give you some peace," she whispered, and he thanked her for the crystal, clutching it tightly as he dropped onto a saggy leather couch. One by one, family visited, and as they filed out, Chase headed back to Tessa's room.

He pushed open the door and slipped inside. Tessa was resting, Christopher tucked to her side, taking his first meal. He moved closer, settled in a chair and watched. Her breast was pale and full as the baby suckled, and he thought she was asleep until she put the baby to her shoulder, gently patting his back. She offered Christopher her other breast, never opening her eyes, and Chase experienced a strange mix of jealousy and contentment just watching them.

"Tessa."

Her eyes flashed open. She made no move to cover herself and it pleased him. Her body was his and primitive instinct told him he'd have it again. He wanted all of her, or nothing, he realized suddenly.

"I *will* see you later." Why did that sound like a threat? He raked his hand through his hair and felt like a stranger to his family. If she'd just smile at him, touch him, he thought. He kissed her forehead, then his son's, his cheek brushing her breast as he did. He heard her gasp and allowed himself a small smile as he left. Cool to him or not, there were some things Tessa couldn't deny.

A nurse caught him before he opened Tessa's hospital room door the next morning.

"Miss Lightfoot asked that I give you this." The portly woman looked uneasy as she handed him a copy of Christopher's birth certificate. Chase was listed as the father. Then exactly what Tessa was doing hit him square in the gut. She was still cutting him out of her life. Why else would she not give this to him herself?

He brushed past the nurse and flung open the door. Tessa looked up from folding clothes into a small suitcase. She was dressed and ready to leave, but Christopher was nowhere in sight.

Panic shot through him like a bullet. "Where's my son?"

She blinked. "In the nursery, of course." Calm and composed.

"I want to see him. Now."

She buzzed the nurse's station. Tessa would never deny Chase his son, but they needed to get a few things clear right now. She couldn't be around him just yet when he saw his son. Not and think straight about their future. "You can see him now, Chase," she said, stalling over her next words. "But I need some more time. Alone." His face drained of color. "I think it's best that we don't see each other for a little while. And that includes—"

"Don't even say it!" Chase cut in, seeing red. In the space of a heartbeat, his patience snapped. "Was this—" he waved the paper "—supposed to make me happy, satisfy me till you got your act together? Offering me a scrap of paper instead of my son? I'm Christopher's father, dammit!"

His rage stunned her. "Calm down, Chase, you're getting out of control."

"Woman, you haven't seen me out of control." He took a step closer, threatening, brandishing the certificate. "This still makes him a bastard."

She gasped and back-stepped, looking as if he'd hit her. *"What!"*

"You heard me. *You* chose to make my son a bastard, Tessa. I've asked you to marry me enough times for you to know exactly how I feel about you. I love you."

Her eyes glossed and she blinked rapidly. "You love the mother of your son."

"How the hell can you stand there and say that?"

"How can I ever be sure it isn't true?" she cried. He

was a madman at just the implication that he'd be parted from his son. What was she supposed to think?

A muscle ticked in his jaw, and his eyes were dark with rage as they pinned her, raked her from head to toe. She'd never seen him like this and remembered what he'd said about his temper. He closed in on her, looming over her, his voice deceptively soft and lethal.

"I've been patient. Goddamn noble. I loved you so much it never mattered what I wanted. Well, I've done it your way, Tessa. Done what was best for *you* long *enough!*" He crumbled the paper in his fist. "Now I do what's best for *my son.*"

"Chase, wait!"

He didn't stop and brushed past a startled nurse. Tessa simply stared at the empty doorway, feeling the floor sinking beneath her feet. How had this happened? She just wanted more time, but now he looked as if he hated her. She sank into a chair as his intention suddenly hit her.

Oh, God. He was going to try to take her son away.

That afternoon Tessa stood in the doorway of her son's room, then looked back over her shoulder at her sisters, Dia and Sam.

"He had a crew in an hour after Christopher was born. They just finished."

Tessa fought back tears, moved to the crib and laid her son on the fluffy mattress. It was exactly like the picture. Everything was here, everything she'd sent back to him.

Till you hold our baby in your arms.

She swallowed and brushed her fingers over her baby's head. He was the image of Chase; already his eyes had that stark, deep blue. How was she going to live seeing Chase in her baby's face every day? But what about what he'd said to her, the threat?

"Tell me he can't take him, Dia."

"I can't. He's done nothing wrong. In fact, his behavior is and was exemplary. The mother usually holds more power in a decision, but no judge will find him an unfit father.''

Tessa knew it before she spoke. God, how had she made such a mess of their lives. She slipped her finger into Christopher's fist, her heart clenching as his fragile grip tightened.

"Come on, Sis," Samantha said, shooting Dia a quelling look, then wrapped her arm around Tessa and pulled her from the room. "You need to get some sleep."

I need to crawl in a hole and die, Tessa thought, moving numbly to her bedroom. She let her sisters pamper her, tuck her in, then she rolled over and cried into the pillow. She loved Chase so much, needed him. She'd had it all and lost it. She'd pushed him too far.

Tessa smiled weakly at Carole Anne and Carl as they fussed over their grandson. Colin sat on the edge of the sofa, making faces and baby talk at Christopher. It was amazing how grown men reverted to idiots when they were around newborns. She couldn't deny them visits, but they had no idea how hard it was. She felt like a hypocrite. The one person who should be in her son's life, wasn't.

Carl looked up, his eyes dark and accusing. "Chase should be here to see this."

Carole Anne nudged her husband sharply, and Tessa looked away. Chase doesn't want to be here with her. Chase only wants Christopher, she thought, and she was constantly tormented by the last words he'd said to her. I loved you enough. *Loved.* Had she crushed it so easily? It proved to her that Chase wanted his son and not her. And her heart threatened to shatter again.

Colin asked to hold Christopher, then scooped up her baby, carefully sitting in a chair. He showed Christopher the stuffed elephant he'd brought, one of several in the two weeks since the birth.

Chase's mother lifted her gaze to Tessa's. "Have you spoken to him?"

Tessa shook her head. The memory of the last time she

saw him, in the hospital, his rage, his fist crushing the birth
certificate as he threatened her, played over and over in her
mind. She was scared to confront him and, mostly, she was
devastated. She'd brought this on herself, hurt him beyond
reason, and she hated herself for it, hated that the memory
of her own parents' arguments kept coming back to haunt
her, make her unsure of his love. Why were you so certain
of your heart three months ago, so certain that you would
die before admitting he didn't love you enough?

Now I do what's best for my son.

She felt doom approach every time she remembered the
wounded look in his eyes. If her misgivings hadn't destroyed him, her refusal to let him into her life would. She
would never deny him Christopher, but he hadn't made an
effort to come see him, either. Or to see her. She couldn't
decide which hurt worse—his threat to do what was best
for their son or this feeling of total abandonment of their
love.

An hour later, Carole Anne and Carl left, yet Colin lingered at the doorway, not ready to give up playing with his
nephew. "It's killing Chase not to see you two, Tessa," he
said suddenly, lifting his gaze from the baby. "You're not
being fair. He loves you so damn much. God, he'll grill me
for an hour when I see him."

It was killing her not to see him, not to see the love he
had for Christopher grow, see him hold his son, talk to him.
Tessa wanted so badly in that instant to call Chase, to invite
him over, but his threats vibrated in her mind, holding her
back. She had to protect herself and her son. She didn't
want to interrogate his brother and make him betray a confidence, but as she took back her son, she had to ask.
"Colin." She hesitated. "Do you know what he's up to?"

Colin arched a brow. "Nothing as far as I know." He
studied her for a moment, his features tightening. "God,
he's got you terrified."

Tessa looked away, rubbing her cheek against Christopher's head.

"He would never do anything to hurt you, Tessa." Colin

shoved his hands in his pockets and shrugged as if he couldn't explain. "He knows exactly what he wants, and he'll get it."

Tessa straightened and looked into Colin's Irish eyes. "So will I."

Chase nestled his son in his arms, rocking him back to sleep after his bottle. He was silently pleased that Tessa had found she couldn't breast-feed for long. It gave him the chance to feed his boy, be with him alone. God, if she knew he was here, he thought, dread racing up his spine. In the distance the phone rang, and after a few moments his mother slipped quietly into the room, her footsteps silent. She didn't have to say that Tessa was coming home. He knew.

For a few minutes he considered waiting, letting her see that no matter what she wanted, he was going to be Christopher's father in every way. He tossed the notion aside quickly, still too hurt by her quick dismissal of their love to confront her. He put his son in his crib, patting his diapered bottom before he left.

Dave nudged Chase.

"Who's that?" Dave said, and the admiration in his tone sent Chase's head up, his eyes narrowing. He straightened immediately as Celeste came toward him, her tiny feet agilely stepping over construction debris. He wiped his hand on his thighs, then grabbed a rag to wipe the sweat from his face and throat. He walked toward her, quickly noting she wrung her hands nervously. His heart rocketed to his throat and threatened his balance.

"Is it Tessa?"

She shook her head. "They're both fine." She hesitated, then said, "Can we talk, Chase, honey?"

He gestured to the shade of a tree, then folded his arms, bracing his shoulder against the trunk. Celeste glanced around, but wouldn't meet his gaze. "You're scaring me, Celeste," he said in a dark voice.

She looked up and her eyes were suspiciously shiny. "This is my fault. This mess with you and my girl."

"Tessa's a grown woman, Celeste. She chose to cut me out."

Almost violently, Celeste shook her head. "I was pregnant with Sam before I married Walter, and for years I based every fight on the fact that he married me for his daughter's sake and not for love."

Chase's features stretched taut.

"I think Tessa remembers what I went through. Even though she was just a little thing." A sob escaped her, and she covered her mouth with her hand. "This is my doing, the ways she thinks now, I mean."

She lifted her gaze and Chase felt cut in half. His harsh expression softened and he gripped her shoulders. "Did you ever change your mind about your husband?"

She looked at him, askance. "Certainly. He made me see that he wanted me first, always had." Her lips curved in a half smile, of memory and lost love. "Walter was a quiet man, but did what was best for his peace of mind first. I expected loud declarations, but I got my assurances in a fierce possessiveness that made other men cringe if they so much as looked at me with desire. He finally admitted that he'd gotten me pregnant intentionally, to keep me."

Chase smiled, wishing he'd known Tessa's father. Yet he felt if he did, there would be a shotgun at his back right now.

"I've tried to reason with her," Celeste was saying. "But she won't even discuss you with anyone."

And she wouldn't even speak to him, refused his calls. Chase reminded himself that he was doing what was best for his son. But deceiving Tessa, sneaking visits with Christopher while his mother was there or her sister, Sam, was tearing at him. He felt as if for the past six weeks he'd been betraying her, but she'd pushed him to going behind her back. His patience was gone, long gone, and Celeste's past had nothing to do with them now.

"She'll have to talk to me soon, Celeste. I can guarantee it."

Tessa stilled as Chase neared, walking across her shop, his hips rocking with his long, smooth gait. Her heart picked up its pace, but he scarcely paid her a glance, passing her and bending immediately to Christopher. From his day swing, her son cooed softly, reaching out to grab his nose, and Chase nuzzled his tummy with his head. Christopher's little arms flailed, a tiny pounding, and Chase laughed deeply.

"Hey, slugger! You're eating well, I see." He kissed him once more, then straightened, and the baby whimpered, tilting his face to look up at the shadow of his father. Tessa frowned, her gaze shooting between them. Christopher hadn't been around him since the birth, but it was as if he knew exactly who Chase was. Was it instinct?

Chase kept the smile plastered on his face and wondered how long he could put up with this act. He was miserable and she wasn't in such great shape, if her gaunt look was any indication.

"Hello, Tessa."

She nodded, clamping a tight grip on her emotions. "Chase."

He missed the sound of his name on her lips. His gaze hungrily swept her from head to toe. "You look great." It was sort of odd, seeing her without a huge tummy. Her clothes, a short, deep purple skirt and matching scoop-neck silk blouse, nipped her figure in all the right places. He could see the hint of her bra, lace and shaping, and he realized it matched the outfit. It was incredibly arousing.

Christopher fussed and Chase dragged his gaze from her and lifted him from the swing. The boy settled quietly against his father and Tessa's throat closed. She would never tire of seeing them together like this.

"He's wet." She reached for the baby as Dana called to

her. "I can manage. See to your customers. Just point me in the direction." After a moment's hesitation that set his teeth to grinding, she nodded to the office. Chase walked into the office, laying Christopher on a small dressing table to change him. A small portable crib rested in the corner, toys and clothes stuffed under the base.

"Whew, son! You couldn't save that one for your mom?" The infant's little mouth opened as if to speak, his legs and arms wiggling. "I guess she gets her share, huh?" With a hand on his son, he gathered the necessary items to attack a diaper dirty enough to bring down Kuwait.

Tessa's fingers tightened on the doorknob as she watched Chase. His moves were swift and sure, but he played with Christopher, nibbling his toes, raining quick kisses over his face. Their baby giggled.

And Tessa felt like the biggest fool.

Three days a week Christopher was here with her in the shop; the other three days were spent between Carole Anne, her mom and Sam until she could find a care-giver worthy of the future president. She'd love to have Christopher with her every minute, but found it hard to get any work done with her son so close, when she wanted to simply settle on the couch and hold him all day.

"Has he been fed?"

Tessa started, focusing her vision on Chase. She nodded.

Chase dismissed her and looked down at his son. "Nap time, kiddo. No, now don't whine. I'll hang around, scare away any bogeymen. You know, dad stuff."

Tessa's eyes burned and her composure sank to a deadly level. She had to be near him, smell him, if she couldn't touch him. She didn't think Chase wanted to even look at her. How had she turned their love into a cold battle so quickly? Even as regret laced through her, it only served to confirm that he wanted his son. And not her. Why else would his love die so quickly?

Chase was all too aware of the woman standing beside him as he laid down his son. He could feel her eyes on him, touching over his body, and he wanted nothing more

than to grab her up in his arms and kiss the daylights out
of her. His groin hardened at the thought of having her
close to him again, of smelling her scent, feeling her body
sheath his. But he was hurting—hurting that she'd allow
his family access to their son and not tolerate a moment
with him. The only reason he'd barreled his way in today
was that he missed Christopher. And he missed the sight
of her over the past weeks. He knew he was risking his
heart every time he looked at her.

"Chase?"

Chase straightened from patting his son into sleep and
stared into her fiery green eyes. "Don't lecture me on my
rights, Tessa."

"I wasn't." She licked her dry lips and his eyes flared.
"How have you been?"

"Rotten." His expression was bland, uncaring, and
Tessa felt her throat tighten.

He covered up his son and turned away.

"Chase, wait."

He faced her, sparing her a painfully mild glance.
"Yes?"

God, he felt miles away from her now. "We need to
talk."

Slowly he shook his head. He couldn't do it, not now.
If he did, he would spill his guts and tell her how mad he
was, how much he was hurting and that she was to blame
for reliving her mother's past at his expense, at the expense
of their love. That he loved her and missed her and hated
her, all in the same breath.

"The only thing I want to hear you say is that you were
wrong."

"We've gone beyond that now."

"We haven't gone anywhere but backward, Tessa."

Her eyes narrowed.

"I was a fool to believe you could love me," he said,
and his voice wavered.

"I do," she whispered, and his posture stiffened.

He scoffed meanly, open wounds driving him. "Well,

you have a strange way of showing it.'' He opened the
door.

"Chase, wait," she called softly. "You can't just walk
away."

"Watch me."

He was gone.

Eleven

Tessa didn't think anything could hurt her more than seeing Chase and having him walk right past her. But when she stepped out of the delicatessen the next day and saw him, farther down the street and heading to his Jeep, they both stilled. His gaze briefly dropped to Christopher, then shot back to her. She couldn't decipher his expression, it was so hard, and she gripped Christopher's stroller handle tighter. Then he climbed into the Jeep and shut the door. Tessa felt the sting of his actions spin through her and she walked briskly toward the park, avoiding eye contact. He wouldn't even take a moment to say hi, to touch Christopher, to talk with her? Good God. Did she need any more proof that she'd lost him?

Chase's gaze shifted over the steering wheel to Tessa walking across the street toward the park. It hurt just to look at her. Six of the longest weeks in his life since Christopher's birth and they were going nowhere. Why wasn't he storming after her and demanding she come to her senses? *Because you keep getting your teeth knocked in, that's why,* he thought. Chase examined his feelings, his methods, and reasoned that he could have gone about the whole matter differently, *if* he didn't love her so much.

Hell, he knew he was a threat to everything she'd worked for and planned so meticulously. He'd walked into her life and turned it upside down. But falling in love hadn't given her the commitment she wanted, and Chase didn't know how much more devoted he could be to her. God, he thought, closing his eyes against the sight of her. He loved her so much. And he knew what she was thinking, the same thing she let torment her for months. *Is it me or the baby he loves? Is his love because I'm the mother of his son? If Christopher weren't here and we'd met under different circumstances, would he love me for just me?* Those questions had tormented him, too, but she didn't see that.

And Christopher would always be there.

Even if he never married her, they would be forever connected through that little boy. And even if they didn't work this out—his chest clenched at the thought—he would *always* be a part of Tessa's life. His fingers flexed on the steering wheel. And from the looks of it, they would just keep hurting each other. Chase's expression withered into utter sadness. He got her love during a tough time in her life, he thought, trying to see things totally from Tessa's point of view. It couldn't have been easy, deciding to have a child without a father, then to do it, only to have him, a man who should have remained anonymous, threaten her world. And now she probably thought he'd take Christopher from her. Even though he loved her too much to do that, he knew that's what she was thinking. And in his hurt, he hadn't corrected her.

She loved him still, Chase didn't doubt. But that love was buried. If she could learn to trust his love for her, he'd see it again. He *had* to keep believing that her distrust was why she didn't want him around. *The heart rules the head and the body rules both,* someone once told him.

He turned his gaze to Tessa and studied her like a painting as she laid his son on a blanket, then unfolded her lunch from a paper sack. A magazine on her lap, she munched on a sandwich as she patted Christopher's diapered bottom. Her back braced against a tree, *their tree,* their spot, she worked off her shoes and crossed her legs at the ankles.

She looked like dessert. Her stomach was flat, her breasts plump and nearly spilling from the fitted blouse. He wanted to unlace the satin strings crisscrossing from her waist up to her breasts and fill his hands with the soft mounds.

But mostly he wanted her to come to him.

His fists clenched, the only sign of the battle waging inside him—his desperation to leave the Jeep and go to her, to tell her he loved her more than his life and that he would do almost anything to have her back in his. Almost. Chase wasn't settling for half a relationship anymore. He wanted all or nothing. His head was ruling this time.

He started the engine and pulled into traffic. He didn't see Tessa rise up on her knees and wave to get his attention, didn't hear her call his name before she resolutely settled back to the blanket and watched him drive away.

The next day, Tessa lifted her son in her arms and hugged him, aching inside, longing for his father to ease the pain she was feeling. She buried her face in his soft neck and inhaled the baby scents. She inhaled again, then frowned as she held up her son, eyeing him.

"You've been conspiring against me, haven't you?"

Christopher blew bubbles, his chubby legs pumping the air.

Tessa hugged him again, then looked across the living room at her elder sister and her mother. "Which one of you is going to confess to letting Chase in here every day?"

Celeste and Samantha paled, looked at each other, then Tessa.

"Christopher smells like his father." She'd been wondering why the scent kept haunting her.

Turning away, she kept her lips from curling into a smile, yet she wanted to shout. She wanted to laugh. Chase was sneaking behind her back to be with his son and it relieved some of Tessa's fears that even his son couldn't hold his love. She'd been wrong about a lot of things. Again. This gave her a little hope as she took her son with her to the bedroom. She dropped onto the bed, snuggling Christopher, and picked up the phone. She dialed Chase's number. It rang and rang, but the answering machine didn't pick up. Frowning, she decided she'd try again later. Chase had said they were done talking. Tessa had other ideas.

Dia gaped at the document. "Is he serious?" she asked, glancing at Tigh, then to Chase's back where he stared out the huge plate glass window.

"I tried, Dia," Tigh said, his expression bearing the battle he'd done with his client long into the night. "He won't budge."

"But this is too far, Chase. You can't do it."

Chase cast a glance over his shoulder, half-lidded and emotionless. His gaze dipped to the custody papers before Dia. "She's given me no choice, Dia. You know that."

"I can't believe it." She shook her head softly, her eyes wet. "I swear if I live to be a hundred, I never thought you'd do *this*."

Chase felt a sharp blade of pain dice him in two. Even the skilled lawyer couldn't see the end to his means.

"This will kill her," Dia whispered, a fracture in her voice as she stared at the papers, searching for the secret hidden within the legal words. "After all you've gone through together. You love her, don't you?" Dia held her breath.

Chase turned from the window, his hands braced behind his back. "More than my life. But she's cut me out of her life, and for what? Because she's afraid I only want her because of our son." His composure slipped a little and he pushed his fingers through his hair, destroying the neat styled look. "She's pushed me to this, Dia. Tessa can't find her heart and I can't wait around for her to do it."

Chase left the room, his own heart shattering with every step. For the hundredth time he hesitated about what he was doing, then he pressed on down the hall. He'd just played his trump card, and if he failed, he'd lose everything.

In her living room, Tessa stared at the thick folded papers in Dia's hand. *Oh, God no, please no,* she thought wildly. He wouldn't. Not Chase.

Tessa's hand trembled as she accepted them. "He did it, didn't he?"

Dia's face was vacant except for the brightness of her eyes. Tessa unfolded the thick document and scanned it. She inhaled sharply and dropped into the nearest chair. Tears welled in her eyes and she swallowed and swallowed and felt her heart about to burst in her chest. Instead it just ripped and tore, gouged by each word she read, bleeding so painfully she couldn't catch her breath. She covered her mouth, air rushing past her fingers.

"Oh, God. Why?"

"Does this really surprise you? You pushed and he folded, Tessa. What can I say?"

"You can tell me how this happened. How you let him do this." She shook the papers in her lawyer's face.

Dia grabbed them. "Get a grip. Hysterics won't help now. What did you think, Tessa? That Chase was going to keep letting you dictate his life and his son's? You've acted like a selfish prima donna, doing what you wanted and needed. He's a man with feelings, for heaven's sake, and he wants what's best for his son and a clean cut from you."

Dia threw the papers into her lap, ignoring the glares from Celeste and Samantha.

"Is someone going to tell us what this is about?" came from Samantha.

"Did he really petition to take Christopher?"

Tessa lifted her face to her mother and sister. "No. He didn't." She swiped at her cheeks with the back of her hand. "He signed away all his rights to Christopher, all claims except for yearly visitations."

Sam sank into a chair with a thump, stunned. Celeste

cried without a sound, tears rolling down her flushed cheeks.

"There is a condition."

Tessa's gaze flew to Dia's.

"You'll notice it's not signed."

Tessa shook her head, confused.

"You have to spend this weekend with him, discussing it, first."

See him? No. She couldn't. She was already dying inside and that would kill her. "I can't. There's a—a businessmen's charity ball this weekend. I have to attend."

"He knows that. *You're* his date."

"No." She shot to her feet, anger spilling from every pore. "I won't. Not after this!"

Dia was in her face, her voice a low growl. "Do it, Tessa, or God knows what he'll be pushed to do next."

"He can't treat me this way!"

"You have exactly what you wanted. Your son. Free and clear of the donor."

"Damn it, Dia. It's not that simple anymore!"

Dia gestured to the papers. "It is to him."

Tessa's eyes narrowed, the document crunching in her fist. "I'll show him just how complicated *this*—" she shook the papers "—can get."

She left the room and Dia folded her arms over her waist, a tiny, satisfied smile on her lips. Her gaze slipped to her sister and, oblivious to their mother, a message passed. Sam's features tightened and she managed a smile. Tessa was going to fight.

Chase carried the bags to the car, then returned to the house, but Tessa was nowhere in sight. He felt strange just being inside the house with her here, since he'd played the sneak for the past two months. She was agreeing to the terms of custody, and even though Chase had put them to her, his hurt ground deeper that she would agree and not fight him. When Dia had called, he had hoped Tessa had refused his offer, hoping that she would be the next call.

But she wasn't. She'd accepted instead that he could easily dismiss his son from his life because of her.

Alone in the living room, he heard movement and soft voices from the back of the house. He glanced around, noticing few changes except for the evidence of a child in the house. Christopher's swing was tucked neatly in the corner, a basket full of his toys beneath; a piece of sheepskin lay spread in the center of the carpet. Chase crossed the room slowly, his fingers kneading a downy blanket tossed carelessly over the arm of a chair, then picking up a set of plastic baby keys.

God, he felt twisted inside and swore the slightest ripple in the air would make him snap. He was no better than the walking wounded, living in his anger, his hurt manifesting into an ugly thing he almost couldn't control. And masked beneath it was his love for Tessa. He buried it, every day shoveling another load of pain on top of it until no one recognized him. She knew where the phone was; she knew where he lived and worked. Why couldn't she see beyond her doubts and come to him? Why couldn't she give him the faith he'd given her? Was he doing all this just to hear her apologize and admit she was wrong?

No. It went deeper, so deep he felt raw inside, and he flinched when Samantha came into the living room, moving silently across the floor, opening her arms to him.

"Chase," she whispered, hugging him. Chase closed his eyes. Sam, he realized, chose no sides. "When I said to be stubborn right back, I didn't mean this."

His mouth quirked briefly as she stepped out of his arms. "She's late."

"Tessa's always late," she said matter-of-factly, and Chase suppressed a smile.

Celeste slipped into the room, Christopher in her arms, and Chase smiled instantly. She held the baby out to him and he gathered his son against his chest, turning away. Sam and Celeste exchanged a frown, but didn't comment.

"Hey, slugger. How's my guy?" Chase nibbled on Christopher's toes as he cooed and shrieked with pleasure.

"God, you've gotten big." He whispered privately to his son, inhaling the sweet baby scents of powder and lotion. He pressed his lips to the top of his head. "Dad's missed you, you know that?"

Tessa stood in the hall entrance, watching. Her heart hadn't stopped racing since she heard him enter the house, and the sight of him in the chic black tuxedo went straight for the jugular. He looked heavenly. And as he held Christopher in his arms, not caring if anything got on his tux, it reminded her that loving was more important to Chase than appearances or another's opinion.

"She's going to make us late," he whispered to his son. "Do you think your mom's ready yet?"

"I am."

Chase looked up, his features pulling tight. Oh, God, he thought. How was he supposed to ignore that! Hell, he knew Tessa was beautiful. And he always saw her in sort of a dainty and seductive way. But this? This was eye-popping glamour. Electric blue crimped silk framed her face like a hood, almost as if the stiff fabric never touched her hair, her skin. It rippled crisply at her throat to offer only a glimpse of golden skin, the airy folds wrapped like a robe and hiding her curves. A satin sash roped her trim waist and she clutched a beaded bag, the frothy cuffs shielding most of her hands. It was captivating and mysterious and Chase's gaze dropped to her legs shimmering in stockings and her tiny feet in matching shoes. He wondered what the hell she had on under it. Yet her hair, styled in a chignon, the wisps falling loosely around her face, brought his attention, any man's attention, to her striking green eyes.

She looked like a chic black cat in a cocoon of blue.

She evoked sex. Pure and raw, and Chase felt the reaction down to his ankles. He didn't even feel Celeste take his son until he was gone. Chase kissed his boy one last time, then nodded to Tessa.

"Ready?"

"Yes. Definitely."

A spear of regret drove into his chest. She was ready to get this over with, he thought, wrapping himself in his hurt.

"Shall we?" she prompted, and Chase frowned into her smile.

Tessa felt her spirits lift a tiny fraction. He couldn't mask his desire for her even if he despised her. She kissed her son, gave last-minute instructions, then proceeded out the door.

Chase was a few steps behind her, watching her walk and telling himself he shouldn't be so intoxicated by the shoosh of fabric beneath the crisp silk. He opened the door and she brushed against him as she slid into the seat. Chase cursed himself for flinching and slammed the car door.

Tessa jumped, her gaze following him as he climbed in and started the engine.

"Are you okay?"

She laid a hand on his forearm and felt the muscles tighten.

Hell no, he wasn't okay. He wanted to take her in his arms and kiss the air right out of her. He wanted to rip that coat off and see what was beneath, but mostly he wanted the crowd in his trousers to leave.

Instead, Chase glared accusingly at her. She's just being pleasant till the papers are signed, he thought. Well, a lot can happen in a few hours, and his signature on the documents was the last of them.

Okay, she thought, so he's going to make this evening difficult. She hadn't expected any less. He looked ready to strangle her, his hurt and rage piercing her with every glance. I love you Chase. I do. Can't you see? Yet they rode in silence like two warlords preparing for battle. As they arrived at the hotel, Chase came around to her side, dismissing the valet and yanking open the car door. He didn't spare her a glance as she swung her legs out of the car.

But his gaze unwillingly dropped to her legs, long and sleek and well muscled, and followed the slight hike of her coat as she touched a foot to the ground. She grasped his hand and stepped onto the curb, then immediately let go. The warmth of his touch lingered on her palm. Cameras flashed wildly and suddenly every reporter in town wanted a shot of her. Chase put a hand to the small of her back and guided her between the velvet ropes inside.

"Good heavens, I didn't expect this!"

"Local coverage, good for donations." His tone was clipped, as if the slightest conversation would choke him.

"And what's the charity?"

His half-lidded gaze slid to her, his lips thin and hard. "Boy's Town."

For boys without fathers or families. Great, she thought. An evening of having the situation rubbed in her face.

Tessa's hopes dropped considerably as they walked through the lobby. His hand on her back felt like a lead weight, heavy and imprisoning. As they entered the banquet room, the festivities were in full swing, dancers moving across the floor, the buffet surrounded by local businessmen. A few paused on their way to the lavish buffet to say hello.

"Tessa." His tone was sharp and she turned, frowning. "Your coat."

Smiling softly, she loosened the sash, her gaze scanning the crowd for familiar faces as she let the coat slide down her arms.

"Oh, God," Chase moaned.

She looked at him, her eyes round with innocence. "Is something wrong?"

"No, nothing." The lie stuck in his throat, threatening to choke him for it.

But her dress drew the attention of every man within forty yards. He had the urge to throw the coat over her and hide her somewhere dark. It was a modernized version of a twenties style, formfitting shift, thin straps, low neckline. Too low. Hell, her breasts were practically pouring over the edge. Then she turned. He got a good look at the back and thought he'd come apart. Fabric draped off her shoulders to scoop so low he could see the curve of her spine, the dip of her waist, and for an instant he wondered how she kept it on. But that wasn't the worst of it. It was covered in beads, shimmering, clear bugle beads that gave the impression of movement even when she was still. The back half of the dress seemed to be cut to shape her bottom, flaring enticingly against the backs of her thighs as she walked. And Chase suddenly realized she was walking away from him.

He strode quickly to catch up with her, grasping her arm. "Where the hell are you going?"

She ignored his viperous tone and laid her hand on his chest, gazing into his eyes. "To get a drink. Would you like one?"

The heat of her touch scalded through the fabric, and Chase stepped back. "No. Our table is number seven." He turned on his heels and headed to it.

Tessa masked her disappointment and continued, stopping to speak with other shop owners, then continuing on to the bar. She didn't normally drink, but decided she needed a little something to give her some courage, however false. She thought she could soften him, reach past their problems and draw back the Chase who loved her so gloriously. She knew the dress was a terribly manipulative thing to use, and from his reaction, which was little more than bland, she was afraid it had failed. But she at least felt beautiful, sexy. Even as much as Chase had insisted she was before, now she felt the power of her femininity. *And* the two hundred crunches she executed daily to get her figure back.

She gave her order to the bartender, feeling the heat of Chase's stare on her spine, its stroke move up to her hair. She stole a look at him over her shoulder, and his blue gaze was like an assault, raking her from head to foot. Tessa smiled tremulously and tugged at her long drop earring. He turned his gaze elsewhere and she felt the cut like a slap. He was tolerating her this evening. But she had other plans. She accepted her drink and headed back to him.

Chase watched her come, her breasts bouncing deliciously with every long-legged step, her dress, that *damn* dress, offering more movement than it should. Chase thought he was going to make an absolute fool of himself and run across the room, punching out every man who looked at her. Because he recognized those glances. It was the "I'd like to see that body naked" look or the "does she make love as good as she moves?" look or the one that made his teeth grind, the "I want her now" look. He knew them all personally. And when several men started to intercept her as she crossed the room, Chase left his chair and met her halfway.

"Did you get what you wanted?"

She frowned at his sudden concern, the softness in his voice evoking memories. What I want is you, she thought, but nodded.

Again Chase placed his hand on her back, guiding her across the floor. It was an utterly possessive gesture and he had no right. Not now, not after the papers had been served, but the temptation of her skin beneath his palm, its smoothness, was more than he could resist.

Tessa swallowed a moan. His touch was almost like coming home and she would have moved closer, but three men blocked their path.

"Chase? Introduce us," a blonde in his late twenties insisted.

God, Chase thought, if he didn't know better he'd swear they were salivating.

"Gentlemen, this is Tessa Lightfoot, owner of—"

"Tessa's Attic," one man finished. "My sister shops there."

"You mean your wife does," another said, and the man flushed red.

They were Chase's competitors and she quickly discovered it went beyond business.

"Didn't you just have a baby?" the blonde asked with a quick, speculative glance down her body.

"Yes, a boy," she said, looking at Chase. "A beautiful

boy." Chase smiled down at her with such unabashed pride she almost forgot the hurt they'd dealt each other.

"So what are you doing here with ugly?" blond and tall asked, nodding to Chase. "You could do much better, Tessa," he said moving closer, his eyes sliding to her breasts, then her face.

Her expression was bland. "With you, I suppose?"

"Oh yeah," he said with feeling, and the suggestion snapped Chase's patience.

"Back off." Chase slid his arm tighter around Tessa's waist. "Miss Lightfoot is my fiancée."

The man winced, shrugging sheepishly as he retreated.

Tessa stared up at Chase and hoped her mouth wasn't hanging open. She didn't dare contradict the man she loved in front of his colleagues, yet her eyes narrowed with swift anger as she agreed. The crowd of admirers quickly dissipated.

"That was unfair, Chase," she hissed the instant they were alone.

His hard gaze slid to her. "Are you on the prowl already?"

"I never was and you know it!" she said through a tight smile.

"I was wondering, with that dress."

"I can take care of myself with those wolves. And your *fiancée?* Was that really necessary?"

His features tightened. "It did the trick."

When he didn't offer more than flippancy, she stopped abruptly and faced him, head-on, her voice a low, angry bite. "It isn't my clothes that are bothering you, is it? You don't want me, but you'll be damned if anyone else will, either."

She didn't give him a chance to comment and asked one of his competitors to dance. Chase stood on the sidelines, not sure what had just happened, and unable to do anything but gather his thoughts and watch her.

She was graceful and exotic and turned several heads as she danced, the glittering fabric shivering over her skin.

When it was over, she didn't return to their table. Chase regretted his comments. This was his last chance. He'd done the unthinkable for her love, to ease his pain and end his suffering. Nightly he'd hoped she was as unhappy as he, but one look at her vibrant smile told him to think again. Yet as she moved around the room, he could pick out her laugh as if he had radar. She was facing him and, briefly, her gaze strayed, locking with his. Chase felt electrified by it and the conversation he was supposed to be involved in seemed to fade away to nothing but Tessa.

Dark possession reared in Chase, a beast screaming inside him. He didn't even offer an excuse to the people talking around him as he left their circle and strode to her.

Tessa's entire body tensed as he neared. He was going to make a scene, she thought, his expression so black and scowling she felt her hands shake. He stopped inches from her, ignored her conversation partners, took her drink and set it on the tray of a passing waiter. Then he caught her hand and pulled her onto the dance floor. He swept her into his arms.

"Chase. That was rude." He held his long frame back from her, bodies inches apart, dignified. But it felt like miles.

"Don't talk. Just dance."

"Go to hell." She tried to step out of his embrace.

He jerked her flush against him. His eyes flared at the contact.

"I am not yours to control."

"No, you prefer that task for yourself."

"You never had to stick around, Chase."

"Yes, I did. Christopher is my son, too."

Not because I love you, she thought, looking away, but for Christopher's sake. Obviously loving his son and loving her were two different things. *Were two different things,* echoed in her head. She lifted her gaze, noticing the hard line of his mouth, the suppressed rage in his expression. It seemed so hopeless.

"Smile," she said through gritted teeth and a fake grin. "We're supposed to be *engaged*."

His expression shifted from shock to realization in the space of a wink. "Oh, yeah." Her legs brushed his, her hips rocking to the music, and Chase remembered what it was like to feel her naked in his arms. He closed his eyes, willing his body to behave. It didn't.

Tessa pretended not to notice.

This is want you wanted, Tessa thought. To be close to him again, to have his attention long enough to take back what she'd lost to her foolishness. *Obviously loving his son and loving her were two different things.* The thought pounced on her over and over, tearing at her composure. She'd known it for a while, it just took longer to understand the price of her misjudgment. The weeks apart from him were hard pills to swallow. For she knew she would have loved Chase even if he wasn't Christopher's father. She loved him for the man he was, not the dad he would be. Even if he chose to walk out of her life and never come back, she would be utterly miserable, but she would still love him with every breath. If she could be certain of this, than why couldn't he? Why hadn't she seen he might be feeling the same way?

When the music softened further, Tessa slid her hand up his lapel, feeling the wild beat of his heart. Look at me, Chase, she silently begged. He did, and she was once again struck with how much she'd hurt him. She had to get him to talk with her rationally.

She gathered her determination and said, "I know you've been visiting Christopher."

His brows shot up.

"Your cologne. He wears it well."

"What are you going to do about it?" She didn't mistake the challenge in his voice.

"Nothing." Her hand slid higher, fingers toying with the curls at his collar, and for a moment, his gaze softened. "I would have let you see him, Chase, anytime, if you'd just asked."

He stopped in the center of the floor, dancers moving around them, but the world, their world, centered on the man locked in her arms. "You didn't want me around, Tessa. At the hospital—"

She pressed her fingers over his lips, silencing him. "I wanted time. I couldn't handle seeing you, then," she whispered. "But I never intended to keep your son from you."

"What did I do to make you hate me so much, Tessa?"

"Oh, Chase," she whispered sadly, then she shook her head. "Not hate, never. Disappointment, maybe."

His features hardened instantly and she felt him tense in her arms. "Who has the right to be disappointed, Tessa? Me, for giving you what you always wanted? Or you, for accepting it?" He stepped out of her arms and headed to their table. Turning, he grabbed her coat, waiting for her to come to him.

It appears, she thought, they were leaving. Good. Because if there was one thing her mother had taught her, it was that a lady didn't do battle in public.

Twelve

Tessa pulled away from his grasp as the valet drove before the hotel entrance. "I swear you turn into the rudest man when you're mad."

"Mad?" He stopped short, absently taking the key from the attendant. "You think that's it?"

She met his gaze over the edge of the open car door. "Of course it's not. Pigheaded, irritating, jealous and stubborn come to mind real quick."

"Describing yourself, Tessa?"

"Hah!" she scoffed and slid into the car, taking clear delight in showing off her legs and the knowledge that his glance, though laced with anger, devoured her.

He moved around the front and climbed into the driver's seat, jamming the key in the ignition and gunning the engine.

"Chase, calm down. I'd like to be alive to see our son grow up."

It was the fear in her voice that stopped him cold. He looked at her and his expression softened a bit. He drove cautiously away from the curb. Inches apart, they rode in silence, Tessa staring out her window, Chase with his eyes on the road. The tension rose with every mile that passed.

When the city was only a glimmer in the distance, she gathered every ounce of courage to open a wound and ask, very softly, "Are you going to tell me where we're going, or just brood?"

"I'm not brooding."

"Of course not."

He shot her a deadly glare.

"Fine, brood. See if I care." Tessa glanced into the back seat, noticing a large cooler and his bags beside hers. And a briefcase. The papers are in there, she thought, and she realized it didn't matter where they were going. Just as long as they were alone. Tessa's mind worked frantically for a way to get him to talk reasonably with her, yet his underlying anger and hurt radiated from him like a warning light to step carefully. He thought she wanted this end, this total exclusion from her life. Well, he was in for a few surprises. She wasn't signing anything. And when he loosened the tie and opened his shirt collar, her attention focused on how seductive he looked, even glaring bullets at her.

She wanted him. Badly. If she lived two centuries, she would always hunger for his kiss, the way his hands felt on her body. She'd thought about it so much in the past hours, she imagined attacking him at the first opportunity. She didn't want to fight. She wanted desperately to postpone the argument, the inevitable torture of emotions they'd suffer discussing him leaving her forever. A knot worked in her throat and she looked at her lap, fidgeting with her purse strap.

Chase glanced to the side and noticed she was biting her lip. She looked scared and his anger softened.

"Tessa, I want you to know—"

"Yes?" she said when he hesitated and her stomach pitched.

"I—I'm sorry." He relaxed visibly. "Back there." He

inclined his head to the city in the distance. "I swear I hated seeing you gawked at by all those men."

"Hated it because of how you feel about me? Or because of the dress?"

Her coat was open, her lush body outlined in the thin garment, and he remembered the hunger in a half dozen men's eyes. "Both," he snapped, and her hopeful expression fell.

Would she ever get through to him?

"I wanted to be with *you*, Chase."

An arrow of hope pierced his chest. "Why? You've ignored me for weeks."

She shook her head. "I called and you didn't answer. Even your answering machine wasn't on."

"I smashed it."

Her eyes widened.

He shrugged, a little sheepish. "I haven't bought a new one yet." He wasn't going to tell her that every day he had come home hoping to find a message there from her and when he didn't, his frustration grew until he took it out on the technology.

"I tried to reach you."

It wasn't enough. "You could have come over, dammit. Or called the office or sent up smoke signals, for Christ's sake!"

"And you could have waited for me to come home just *one* of those times when you were in my house."

"I got tired of always hunting you down!"

"Jeez, are you going to keep verbally beating me or would you rather just deck me one and get it over with?"

He looked horrified. "Hell, no!"

"Well, right now, you look mad enough to tear me in half."

"Well, I'm not!"

She arched a brow at that.

"I'm—" he hesitated "—hell, I don't know what I am," he rasped in frustration, pulling to a sharp halt in front of a cottage and shutting off the motor.

"Me, either," she whispered under her breath as he left the car to open the back and retrieve their bags. "But I will."

A smile ghosted across her lips as she followed, waiting on the porch as he brought the cooler and the bags inside. She looked outside, then inside. It was quaint and rustic. "Humm." She stepped inside. "Quiet, isolated."

"So?" Lord, he sounded like a school-yard bully.

"This is good."

"Why?" He shut the door, hard.

She tossed her handbag on a nearby side table and let the silk coat slip from her body and onto the floor. Chase's gaze raked her, his dark expression creasing deeper as she strolled closer.

"Why," he repeated, softer. She was so close her breasts gently pressed against his shirt, a soft cushion of temptation and desire, and his body reacted swiftly.

"Because—" She grabbed his lapels, yanking him down to meet her face. His eyes flared. "We're going to make *a lot of noise.*" Her mouth covered his, grinding against his lips, and she didn't stop.

Chase moaned, clutching her in his arms and returning her kiss over and over. The uncapping of sudden desire rocked him to his heels. Her kiss was heavy and penetrating, her mouth wide, her tongue thrusting and teasing in the same sweep. Chase unleashed his frustration, his hands roughly mapping her body from shoulder to thighs, his mouth a hard slash across hers.

It was a battle to see who would surrender.

Neither did.

He cupped her bottom and jerked her against his hard need. She moaned and shoved the jacket off his shoulders, tore at the studs on his shirt. They scattered to the floor like tacks. Chase did what he'd been aching to do all night and covered her breasts with his hands. She whimpered against his mouth, gripping his belt and unleashing the leather, flipping a button, then pushing the zipper down. His kiss grew harder. She jerked his shirt free, molded the bare skin of his stomach, and the heat and fire between them grew to dangerous heights. He shoved the straps off her shoulders, bending her back over his arm as he dragged the fabric down. His lips closed over her bare nipple.

"Oh, God." She clutched his head, sliding her hands beneath his stiff shirt, shoving it down and wishing he was naked and inside her. He devoured her breast, drawing her nipple deep into the hot suck of his mouth, then scraping his teeth across her skin and suckling its mate. "You know where this is going," she managed, breathless as she ran her hands wildly over his chest and down his stomach.

His muscles jumped. "I hope so." He smiled against her nipple, flicking his tongue wildly over the taut peak, and she writhed in his arms. "I have protection."

"Not necessary." She gasped, her hand dipping beneath his waistband, shoving frantically at his trousers and briefs. "Oh, Chase." Her hand encircled him. "You're so warm."

"And hard. I know." Her fingertips slid over his hardness. "Angel, angel. I can't wait."

She met his gaze. "Then don't."

The sound of their breath and the slow slide of her zipper filled the room.

"I've been thinking about doing that all night." They sank to the floor.

She opened for him, pulling him between her thighs. He rocked against the heat of her, fabric the only barrier. He wanted it gone. Now. And in quick movements, he shoved her dress up, hooking his thumbs in the sides of her panties and twisting the thin strip around his fist. Savagely, he yanked and the delicate fabric snapped. Her eyes flared. He dragged the scrap from her, dangling it like a trophy before tossing it over his shoulder.

She freed him from his trousers and he plunged into her with a force that drove her across the floor, and Tessa met him, her hips slamming back. She knew he'd held back for her in the past, but this time, Tessa felt the full power of Chase's passion.

It was raw and dark, his body driving and driving, his

mouth consuming hers. His fingers plowed into her hair as his body filled hers, harder and harder, and her legs clutched him, begging for more. And he gave it.

Chase couldn't stop himself. He'd hungered for her for so long, loved her so much, and his frustration and hurt and need, his *need,* spilled over into his touch. He knew he was rough, but she urged him on, her hands erotic and probing, her teeth scraping his flesh, nipping his shoulder. She was hot and slick and pulsing, her breath ragged and he felt her tense and tense—then it came. The wild storm of sensation, the flex of slick muscles surrounding his arousal, the convulsions of her desire swamping him like a hot rain. Chase held her gaze as he drove into her, burying himself deeply, mashing tighter and tighter. Splintered pleasure drenched them in a place only they could reach.

She bucked against him and he rode the pulse, a harsh, guttural groan rumbling in his chest, her name on his lips. The incredible scent of her washed over him and he covered her mouth with his, swallowing her sighs, kissing her long after the last tremor faded.

They said nothing. But Chase remained inside her, still hard, still wanting the world and their problems to go away. She stroked his hair, fingers sifting, and Tessa felt tears trickle from the corner of her eyes and dampen her hair. A small smile curved her lips.

He lifted his head to look at her.

"I love you, Tessa."

Another tear escaped. She cupped his face in her palms. "I love you, too," she whispered over the rock in her throat. "I do."

He brushed his mouth over her lips, her eyes, then slowly left her body, standing to strip off his clothes. His eyes never left hers. He loved watching her watch him. Then he stripped her naked, taking great pleasure in removing the garterless stockings, nibbling her toes before pulling her into the circle of his arms. They stayed on the floor though a bed was only a room away.

He lit a fire in the hearth, carrying her before it and

dragging a quilt from the sofa. He tossed it over them both. Chase pillowed his head on her lap, Tessa toying with his hair. He was too contented to move, he thought. Or talk about what needed to be said. He was drained. Smiling softly, he managed to turn his head to look at her. Her breasts were bare to his gaze, her eyes closed. Her neat chignon was a wild, sexy tangle. He would never have thought Tessa could be so wonderfully demanding. It was clear he still had a lot to learn about this woman.

"I bet I have scratches on my back."

She smiled, almost smug, but didn't open her eyes. "I bet you woke the dead with that yell."

Slowly he dragged the quilt down, exposing her flesh, the dark triangle between her thighs. He ran his finger along the edge of dewy flesh and she flexed beautifully. Chase pushed open her legs and rolled between. His gaze held with hers as he dipped his head. His tongue stroked across her and he chuckled darkly as she flopped back with a moan.

Chase devoured her, and it was Tessa who woke the spirits with her cries of pleasure.

Long before dawn Chase carried her to the bedroom, wrapped in the quilt. She snuggled under the covers, reaching for him, pulling him around her body. Chase had missed this, and his hands couldn't keep still, every touch reveling in the feel of her skin. He rediscovered her figure without his child inside her, the heaviness of her breasts, the flare of her hips, and he made love to her again, slowly, tenderly, telling her without words that it would always be like this, that he would always love her and need her. If she wanted it.

She did, and Tessa lavished him with her love as he made good on a long-ago whispered promise—to love her anyway he could imagine and never stop. They were gentle and slow, then wild and raw with passion, but neither spoke of the custody papers, of the hurt they'd dealt each other over the weeks. With their bodies they sought healing and rebirth and in each other's arms they slept the sleep of contentment, avoiding the inevitable. Avoiding dawn.

Chase smelled coffee and opened his eyes, squinting against the light streaming through the window. He was alone and a cup rested on the nightstand, daring him to take it and face the day.

He didn't want it. He wanted Tessa to come back to bed and make love with him again. God, she was a wild creature, he thought, sitting up and swinging his legs over the side. He noticed their bags on the floor, hers open and riffled. And the sexy lingerie spilling from the leather case. He knew what she was up to, the little witch. Wild loving would soften him, make him palatable. It did, but part of it kept him from giving in to what he needed to say to her. He wanted to hold these moments a little while longer, Chase thought, bringing the coffee cup to his lips, then realized she was standing in the doorway, leaning against the frame.

"Hi."

She let her gaze slide over his bare chest and lower, to where the sheets pooled around his hips. Chase felt himself harden instantly. It had a lot to do with the deep maroon lace bra and skimpy thong panties she wore. He recognized them from the sets she'd been trying to dig out of the box in the storeroom, the first time he'd experienced her passion. The look in her eyes said she remembered, too.

"I thought you said you couldn't get a thigh into that."

"I guess I was wrong." The few words spoke volumes, yet she didn't come to him. "Chase?"

"Yeah?" He dragged his gaze from the lush display of her body to her face.

"Now that I have your complete attention," she said with a smile while reaching for a matching silk robe and slipping it on, "we need to talk."

Chase's heart shot to his throat and he leaned his back against the headboard, drawing up one leg beneath the sheet and resting his coffee cup on his knee. Inside he was suddenly a mass of cut nerves. "It that why you attacked me on the doorstep? To get my attention?"

Her skin deepened with color. "It was a spontaneous decision. Since you've avoided me like the plague for weeks now—"

"Me?" He sat up a bit. "You're the one who insisted we shouldn't see each other."

She eyed him meaningfully, yanking on her robe sash. "I didn't mean permanently, Chase."

"Could have fooled me," he groused. He took a fortifying sip of coffee.

"I tried to talk to you, in the hospital, in the shop, but you just kept walking away and building a bigger wall. What was I supposed to do?"

He toyed with the cup handle, then set it aside and met her gaze. "Bust it down, maybe."

She pressed her knee to the bed, then settled on the edge, hands on her lap. "I would never have denied you time with Christopher."

"No," he scoffed, glancing away. "Only with you." He made a frustrated sound and met her gaze, months of hurt in his eyes. "I felt like an outcast, Tessa, and after Christopher was born, I felt as if everyone else was invited into your life, except me. Do you know how much that hurt?" His fist bunched in the sheets. "That you couldn't stand a minute around me?"

"Oh, Chase," she cried softly. "All I could do was *feel* your emotions, how much I was hurting you by not marrying you, and how much I loved you despite the uncertainty and fear I felt." Her eyes dampened, shined. "I wanted you with me every second, but I couldn't think with you around. You badgered me every day just by proposing. And I never wanted to feel as vulnerable and weak as Ryan made me feel."

"I'm not Ryan!" he exploded, lurching from the bed, naked. Stunned by his angry burst, Tessa watched as he grabbed a pair of shorts from his duffel, jamming them on.

When he looked as if he'd walk out, she blurted, "My mom was pregnant with Sam before she married Dad—"

He looked up from fastening his shorts. "She told me."

She was startled, then frowned. "Did she tell you that they argued for years over whether he married her for Samantha's sake or for love, that he would storm out and not come back for days and she'd cry herself to sleep?" Chase shook his head. "I hated him for making her feel so rotten. I didn't want that for us."

"You're not your mother, Tessa," he bit out, his eyes sharp. "And I'm not your dad." He left the room and she chased him, catching hold of his arm.

"I know." He wouldn't look at her and she could feel every cell of his capped pain. "But can you see what I've been fighting?"

He gave her a half-lidded glance. "All I see is a woman hiding behind some childhood memory that has nothing to do with us," he said, pulling free. "And she still doesn't know what she wants." He strode out the open French doors and onto the sun deck.

"I want you!" she called, then followed. "I want you," she said again, softer.

Gripping the railing, Chase stared down at the dark water. "How can *I* believe you?" he said, then pushed away to face her. "Don't you think I had fears? Hell, Tessa, you didn't even need me to get pregnant with my baby. You certainly didn't need me to give birth. You didn't need me to be around at all." He flung his hands out in a helpless gesture. "Ever." Looking somewhere beyond her, he clenched his fists at his sides, veins and muscles flexing as he said, "You did everything without me, didn't want my help, and for a while there," his gaze collided with hers, his anger erupting, "I felt like some security blanket you snuggled with then discarded when you got yourself together!"

She gasped and stepped back. "That isn't true!"

"Isn't it?"

"No! For God's sake, Chase. Just because I'm self-reliant doesn't mean I don't need you."

He scoffed. "You've dictated this relationship. Organized it into a nice little square where you could deal with it on your terms, in your own time. Well, I've got news for you, Tessa Lightfoot. I'm a round peg. And I don't fit."

Fear struck through her. "What are you saying?"

"I'm saying I don't want to be second to your unfounded fears and your need for...independence."

She planted her hands on her hips and gave him a cocky look. "Look who's talking. You bullied me from day one, Chase Madison. And need I remind you that *you forced* your way into my life and threatened everything I'd struggled over for years." She shrugged, palms out. "Of course, I held on to it. Half because it was the only security I had, except our baby, and half because I was afraid that what I really wanted...wasn't real."

He blinked as understanding struck, then his eyes narrowed, distrusting the calm in the storm. "And what makes you so sure you know what you want now?"

There was a stretch of silence before she said, "Because what I have isn't enough."

He folded his arms over his naked chest and waited for more.

"Because loving you and loving our child are two different things."

"Surprise, surprise," he muttered, looking off to the side.

She moved up to him, against him. "Chase?"

"Yeah." He wouldn't look at her and she pressed her hand to his cheek and made him.

"I've missed you terribly."

He crumbled, his shoulders sagging, arms falling to his sides.

She closed her hands around his muscled biceps. "I need you to love me, Chase." Her searching eyes filled with tears. "Nothing in my life means anything except having you there, every hour, every minute." Her voice lowered to a husky pitch, fracturing with torment. "I feel so broken inside without you."

Chase gazed down into her bright green eyes and saw her heart pleading for his understanding. Slowly his arms slipped around her waist, pulling her flush against him. He smoothed his hand up her back and tucked her head against the curve of his shoulder. "Now you know how I've been feeling for the past months."

"I'm sorry I hurt you."

Her quiet tears wet his bare chest. "Yeah, me too."

"I love you, Chase." She squeezed him tighter. "That never stopped."

"I know, angel," he said softly. "I love you."

Over her head, his gaze rested on his briefcase, the papers he knew were inside, and he took a deep breath, hoping he wasn't putting a gun to his future. He let her go and moved to the case, flipping the latches and opening it. His hand hesitated.

"Chase?"

He turned, the document crimping in his hand.

Her complexion paled as her gaze dropped to the papers, their every word imprinted in her brain. Oh, God. *They were signed.* She spun away, covering her mouth to hold back a cry as she flew down the steps to the pier. She stopped, unable to go farther, and felt him move up behind her. She looked at him over her shoulder.

"I thought we'd gone past that." Her voice was scarcely a whisper.

Chase winced, hearing her torment in every syllable, but he clung to his need to clear away the last bit of rubble between them. "Not far enough."

She faced him and stared at the document, swiping her tears with the sleeve of her robe. That he even had them, let alone *signed* them, was so far removed from his supposed feelings that she was struck dumb again.

Her gaze lifted to his. "Why are you doing this still?"

"Because I want to see you completely happy."

She choked, aghast. "And you think this will do it?"

she cried, looking as if he'd stabbed her, and Chase grasped for his equilibrium. "Chase, we're a—"

"Family?" he cut in, arching a brow. "I want to be a husband, a lover...then a father."

The pier bobbed beneath her bare feet as she rapidly searched his stark features. "You love our baby."

He reared back. "Of course I do," came without a doubt. "I gave up my rights, but not my heart. I love you, Tessa," he said, advancing and making her back-step down the dock. "*You*. Because you're gentle and caring and you're the sexiest woman on this earth." He seared a quick look down her body. "Not because you suffered having our baby. I can't separate the woman who carried my child from the woman I love." He shrugged. "They have the same body, the same heart. I have no rights." He snapped the thick document against the wind. "I gave them away to prove it's you I want. *You* I love first." He leaned down in her face, his voice softening a fraction. "When Christopher is grown and gone, it'll still be just you."

Confused, her shoulders drooping, Tessa stared up into the eyes of the man who could destroy her world. "Now what do we do?"

Chase looked at the sky and muttered, "Damn," then met her gaze. "For a smart woman, you act incredibly stupid far too often."

She gasped, openmouthed, and he gave her a shove, sending her tumbling backward off the dock and into the water. She burst through the surface, shoving her hair from her face and glaring at him. She struggled to keep afloat in the waterlogged robe, and Chase, the rat, simply sat on the edge of the pier, holding out his hand.

"All you have to do is take it, Tessa. Come to me."

"You hurt me!" she cried. "You scared me!"

"I know, angel," came regretfully. "And now I'm being selfish, so don't come to me because of Christopher. Don't come to me because we're good together and making love with you is like a flash fire. Come to me because I'll die without you." He slipped into the water, paddling out to her. "Be magnanimous and feel sorry for me 'cause I don't want to be a part of your life, even for our son's sake, if I can't have every part of you to love."

Her tears mixed with droplets of water and they stared and stared. Then suddenly Tessa sank under the surface, emerging before him, her body brushing his. Chase gazed into her green eyes, his heart beating so fast he swore it would burst from his chest any second.

"Tessa?"

She wrapped her arms around him and felt him tremble. That he would risk everything for her, to erase all final doubts, made her love him more than she'd thought possible. "Poor, lonely man," she whispered. "Feel sorry for *me,* Chase. Take pity on *me.* I couldn't see what I had till it was gone. I feel like such an idiot."

"Stubborn, scared and a little too self-reliant for my ego to take, maybe." The teasing went out of his voice and his expression. "But I was never gone, angel." He smoothed the hair back from her face, his eyes suspiciously bright. "Just waiting."

"Marry me, Chase. Please."

He choked a laugh. "'Bout time you asked, woman. I was running out of ways to get back into your heart."

"You never left." She cupped his face in her hand and shook him a bit. "God, I'm so glad you stuck around, Chase Madison!" He grinned his sappy grin. "I think I knew you would since the day you waited on crabby Miss Dewberry." Her mouth neared, tempting him.

"You could've come around before now," he groused good-naturedly.

She scoffed, denying the kiss. "And blow your supreme confidence bigger than it is? I don't think so."

He laughed, hugging her. "Bothers you, doesn't it? That *I* was right about us."

"No." Her eyes softened and her words warmed his lips. "But you can keep thinking that if it makes *you* happy."

The petition floated by and Tessa grabbed it, ripping it

into pieces as Chase backstroked toward the shore, Tessa lying across his body.

"Let's go home and tell our son."

"Later," he growled, drawing her on the soft shore, immediately covering her body with his. "I want to make certain his momma knows how babies are *really* made."

She arched a brow, working his cutoffs open. "Making up for lost time?"

"No, angel," he whispered against her lips as he tore at her panties. "Making a lifetime."

"What a wonderful start." The last word came in a breathless rush as Chase filled her, their love flowing around them as they slid sweetly into heaven.

Epilogue

Five years later

Chase watched his wife settle to the edge of the dock, her feet in the water. Tessa was still slim after three children, and they'd decided that was all they could handle. All boys. All with energy to spare. Often she told him she wanted a girl just so she wouldn't feel outnumbered. Suddenly she hopped into the water, splashing him, then swimming out to the kids.

"Momma ride!" Their three-year-old begged, arms out, his life jacket making him look like an orange buoy.

Tessa pulled Chance from the boat and onto her back, swimming back to the dock. She gripped the edge. "Somebody's tired." She inclined her head.

"You mean the dad?" Chase asked.

She made a face. "Here, take this lug. God, he's heavy."

Chase grasped Chance and bobbed him in the water. He kicked wildly, then whined. "I'll put him down." Chance's lower lip curled pitifully and Chase sent him a warning glance. "No. Nap first, pal." He looked at her. "How about those guys?"

"In a bit. I want to play."

He chuckled, stood and walked back down the pier, distracting Chance from his inevitable nap by swinging him down between his legs and back up into his arms. The baby squealed and begged for more, and Chase groaned, looking back over his shoulder. Tessa gave him that I-told-you-not-to-wind-him-up look.

"Hey, Mom!" Christopher called, sliding his legs over the edge of the boat. "Race you." He and his brother Casey were the spitting image of their father; only Chance had her green eyes and black hair.

"Sure. To the rope." Chris dropped into the water and swam as if a shark was on his heels. Tessa couldn't catch him if she tried. He grasped the rope and climbed it halfway, waving wildly.

Chase came out of the cabin, sans a child, and she frowned as she swam back to the pier. "My mom," he said, inclining his head to the house.

"Wimped out, huh? You just didn't want to deal with it. You gave him the donuts this morning and let him O.D. on sugar."

"I know, but I get tired of that pouting lip of his. It makes me feel like a creep." He settled beside her and she propped her arms on the floating dock, gazing up at her husband. Christopher yelled for his attention and he gave it, watching his son swing on the rope, then drop into the water.

"God, he's all arms and legs."

"So are you, nice ones."

He looked down at her, a secret smile passing between them. "Think anyone will ever figure out why we bought this place?"

"Do you care?"

She hung onto his legs, hers gently moving to keep herself afloat. Her breasts pushed against the tight black tank suit. His body remembered every moment he'd spent loving her and announced it to the world.

She noticed.

"You have that look in your eyes again, Tessa."

"What look?" came with mock innocence.

"The same one when you let me catch you last night."

"I didn't *let* you catch me."

"Liar." With three boys, their nightly walks were their only uninterrupted time together.

Their children laughed and Chase gazed at them with such overpowering love, Tessa lost her breath. She'd never known a man who could love so much.

"God, I'm glad I found you, angel," he said, then looked down at her.

This man wore his heart on his sleeve, she thought happily. "Well, a certain part of you found me. Three times."

He leaned close, grasping her arms and pulling her from the water. He draped her across his lap as if their entire family weren't watching and getting a good laugh at their expense. "I love you, angel."

"I love you, too." She stroked the side of his face, his mouth nearing hers, a breath away.

"Hey, Dad. Dad! *Dad!*" Christopher called when he didn't answer in the preferred three seconds.

"Yeah?" Chase didn't look up.

"Quit smooching and come play."

"I *am* playing, son," Chase said, and laughter erupted around them.

"Daaaad!" Both boys chimed.

Tessa arched a brow and Chase groaned, pressing his forehead to hers. His disappointment was great for her ego.

"There wasn't anything about lack of attention for the dad in those child-rearing books, you know."

Her lips twitched at his sour expression. "They're your sons."

"Convenient for you." His gaze dropped meaningfully to the bulge in his swim trunks. "Now."

"Hey. You wanted to be a dad, Chase Madison."

Clearly the blame was on him and his run to the doughnut store today. And he shouldered it willingly, grinning as he dumped her into the water. She came up sputtering. Christopher and Casey's giggles floated across the water like soft music.

"I should have seen that coming," she muttered, swiping water from her face.

He slid into the water. "I was hoping you'd say that." Chase wrapped his arms around her, letting her feel what she did to him, his gaze telling her their walk would be very long tonight. He wiggled his brows. She laughed and used his body to push off.

"That's *if* you can catch me," she called, then dived under the water.

Casey clapped. "Get her, Dad! Get her!"

"Over there, Dad!" Christopher pointed.

"Thanks, guys." He dived underwater, wondering if their mother knew how much they ganged up on her. Chase snared her ankle, yanking her into his arms and kissing her as they rose to the surface.

"You're 'posed to dunk her!" Christopher shouted, then giggled when his mom sent him a warning glance.

"Meet me on the porch after bedtime," she said against his lips, "and we'll make the trees shake."

Chase groaned at the image, sinking into her mouth just as two impatient boys cannonballed inches from them.

They broke apart and Chase looked at Tessa, a frown on his face.

"They're your sons," she warned gently. "Deal with it."

Chase watched her swim away, enjoying the sound of her laughter, laced with sensual promise. His boys clung to him like monkeys and as much as he adored them, he was going to tucker them out so she could keep that promise. Now and for the next couple of centuries.

*   *   *   *   *

SILHOUETTE

Desire®

COMING NEXT MONTH

NOBODY'S CHILD Ann Major

Children of Destiny

Cutter Lord had always secretly loved his brother's wife, Cheyenne, but her loyalties had been to her husband and son. Then her husband was murdered and her child kidnapped. Now Cutter had to rescue her son; after all, he was the boy's father...

JOURNEY'S END BJ James

The Black Watch

Merrill Santiago had retreated to Ty O'Hara's isolated ranch for some peace and quiet... Instead, the beautiful agent found Ty to be the most dangerous man she'd ever met because he threatened to tear down all her defences.

HOW TO WIN (BACK) A WIFE Lass Small

Tyler Fuller still loved his ex-wife, Kayla, and, having grown tired of spending the long, cold nights alone, he vowed to win her back. But Kayla wanted to take things slow...and Tyler was amazed to discover just how good slow could be...

THE BRIDAL SHOWER Elizabeth August

Always a Bridesmaid!

When Michael Flint learned that Emma Wynn was about to marry another man, he was determined to stop her. She'd turned down his proposal before, but Michael *would* get his 'yes' this time...

LONE STAR KIND OF MAN Peggy Moreland

Wives Wanted!

Years ago, Reggie Giles had loved Cody Fipes...and begged him to run away with her. But Cody had said no and gone off to seek his fortune. Now they're both back and Cody doesn't want to let Reggie go—ever again!

ANOTHER MAN'S BABY Judith McWilliams

Ginny Alton had agreed to impersonate her cousin and travel thousands of miles with her cousin's baby. On arrival, Ginny was met by Philip Lysander who decided to pretend to be the baby's father...and Ginny's lover...

On sale from 22nd May 1998

COMING NEXT MONTH FROM

 **SILHOUETTE®**

Sensation
A thrilling mix of passion, adventure and drama

MIND OVER MARRIAGE Rebecca Daniels
LOVING MARIAH Beverly Bird
PRIME SUSPECT Maggie Price
BADLANDS BAD BOY Maggie Shayne

Intrigue
Danger, deception and desire

ANGEL WITH AN ATTITUDE Carly Bishop
FATHER AND CHILD Rebecca York
THE EYES OF DEREK ARCHER Vickie York
STORM WARNINGS Judi Lind

Special Edition
Satisfying romances packed with emotion

ALISSA'S MIRACLE Ginna Gray
THE MYSTERIOUS STRANGER Susan Mallery
THE KNIGHT, THE WAITRESS AND THE TODDLER Arlene James
THE PRINCESS GETS ENGAGED Tracy Sinclair
THE PATERNITY TEST Pamela Toth
JUST JESSIE Lisette Belisle

On sale from 22nd May 1998

DEBBIE MACOMBER

The Playboy and the Widow

A confirmed bachelor, Cliff Howard wasn't prepared to
trade in the fast lane for car pools. Diana Collins lived life
hiding behind motherhood and determined to play it
safe. They were both adept at playing their roles.
Until the playboy met the widow...

"Debbie Macomber's stories sparkle with love and laughter..."
—*New York Times* bestselling author, Jayne Ann Krentz

1-55166-080-6
AVAILABLE NOW IN PAPERBACK

To celebrate the 15th Anniversary of the Desire™ series we're giving away a year's supply of Silhouette Desire® books—absolutely FREE!

10 prizes of
FREE Silhouette
Desire books
for a whole year.
★ PLUS ★
100 runners up prizes of a
stunning Austrian crystal
pendant on a beautiful
golden chain. Simply enter
our Celebration
competition
today for your
chance to win!

Overleaf there are twelve words listed, each of which is hidden in the word grid. All you have to do is find all the words in the grid and circle them. When you have completed the puzzle, don't forget to fill in your name and address details in the space provided below, pop this page into an envelope (you don't even need a stamp) and post it today. Hurry—the competition ends 31 August 1998.

Are you a Reader Service™ subscriber?   Yes ❑   No ❑

Ms/Mrs/Miss/Mr ....

Address ....

....

....Postcode..........................

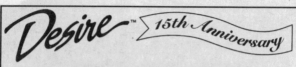

Desire — 15th Anniversary

FREE COMPETITION

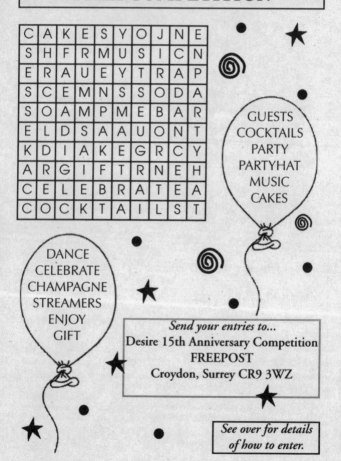

C	A	K	E	S	Y	O	J	N	E
S	H	F	R	M	U	S	I	C	N
E	R	A	U	E	Y	T	R	A	P
S	C	E	M	N	S	S	O	D	A
S	O	A	M	P	M	E	B	A	R
E	L	D	S	A	A	U	O	N	T
K	D	I	A	K	E	G	R	C	Y
A	R	G	I	F	T	R	N	E	H
C	E	L	E	B	R	A	T	E	A
C	O	C	K	T	A	I	L	S	T

GUESTS
COCKTAILS
PARTY
PARTYHAT
MUSIC
CAKES

DANCE
CELEBRATE
CHAMPAGNE
STREAMERS
ENJOY
GIFT

Send your entries to...
**Desire 15th Anniversary Competition
FREEPOST
Croydon, Surrey CR9 3WZ**

*See over for details
of how to enter.*